A SKULL IN SHADOWS LANE

A SKULL IN SHADOWS LANE

Robert Swindells

First published in Great Britain 2012
by Corgi Books
This Large Print edition published 2012
by AudioGO Ltd
by arrangement with
The Random House Group Ltd

ISBN: 978 1445 894287

British Library Cataloguing in Publication Data available

Printed and bound in Great Britain by
MPG Books Group Limited

I dedicate this book to the many, many people who have played their parts in making my career a happy and successful one: my agent, editors past and present, copy editors, sales reps, and everybody who's put up with my nonsense and done the real work while I've swanned around playing the sensitive artist and getting all the glory. Oh—and I mustn't forget my young fans, because without them I'd be sitting in a doorway somewhere with a plastic cup and a dog. To every one of you, my heartfelt thanks.

ONE

OOH, GOODY

'I suppose it's a good thing,' said Josh, 'the war being over, but . . .'

'I know what you're going to say,' put in his sister Jinty, as they stood by the village pond, watching ducks. 'The American flyers don't shell out chewing gum and candy like they did. There's no blackout, sirens or shelter-drill, and no spies to spy on. You were going to say it's boring, and you're right.'

Josh nodded. 'I don't know what kids found to do before the war, Sis. Nothing ever happens in Coney Cley.'

Jinty was eleven; a skinny, lively girl with short blonde hair. Josh was a year younger, and the quiet type. He liked books and nature, but secretly wished he was a hero like his dad.

The war had lasted six years, so neither of them remembered much about the time before. Their dad was a shadowy figure now: a big, amiable presence who'd laughed a lot and dug the garden. He'd joined the army and gone off to fight, and that must've made a huge difference to Mum's life, but the children couldn't remember noticing at the time. They remembered the telegram, though: the one that came two years ago and made Mum howl. It was their sharpest memory, the first time they'd seen a grown-up person cry. 'Daddy won't be coming home to us,' she'd said later, when Grandma had come from Stowmarket with a suitcase to stay with them for a while.

'There's the haunted house,' said Jinty. '*That* was there before the war, I bet kids used to go there.'

Josh pulled a face. 'I don't think it's haunted at all. Not with a name like Cornflower Cottage. What sort of name's *that* for a haunted house? It's more like something in *Sunny Stories*.'

Jinty chuckled. 'Well, go on then: what *would* be a good name for a haunted house, Josh?'

'Oh, *you* know.' He frowned. 'Black

2

Bat Manor, Hangman's Grange, Dead Cat Vicarage. Something like that.'

'Dead Cat *Vicarage*?' hooted his sister. 'How would it get *that* name, you chump?'

'Well, one day a cat got inside this vicarage, and the vicar didn't notice. He went out, locking the door behind him. Half an hour later he collapsed and got carted off to hospital. He was gone six weeks. When he came out of hospital and opened the vicarage door, the cat was draped across the doormat, crawling with maggots. It had starved to death. So for ever after, people called it Dead Cat Vicarage.'

Jinty shook her head. 'I swear you're a lunatic, Josh Linton. And anyway, Cornflower Cottage is in Shadows Lane, which definitely *isn't* a *Sunny Stories* sort of name, and I vote we go down there on Saturday and have a dekko.'

Her brother shrugged. 'If you like, but I'd rather be up at the air base saying, "Got any gum, chum?" to a Yank, like in the good old days. You can't hang about near the gates now, because of those guards in black who don't speak English.'

Jinty nodded. 'DPs—displaced persons. They're Poles and Ukrainians who lost everything in the war. They have no home, so the Yanks give 'em jobs as guards and cooks and labourers. So you see, the war *wasn't* the good old days for most people, Josh. Including Mum. I'm off to help her set the table—it's stuffed cabbage for dinner.'

'Ooh, goody,' growled Josh.

TWO

HORRID BOY

'One two is two, two twos are four, three twos are six, four twos—'

'Are you *chewing*, Victor Hammond?'

'No, miss, sucking.' The chant broke up as Miss Bowman strode between rows of desks to grab a handful of Victor's hair.

'*Sucking?*' she screeched, lifting the

4

lad from his seat by it. 'In *my* arithmetic lesson? Come out here, you rude, impudent boy: come *on*.' She yanked him towards the wastepaper basket that stood beside her desk and made him bend over it. 'Spit it out at once, you *horrid* boy.'

Victor hawked as loudly as he could and spat a soggy wad of liquorice root into the basket. The teacher pulled a disgusted face, and keeping her grip on his hair with one hand, began slapping the backs of his legs with the other. Victor was a big lad. As Miss Bowman slapped he moved, trying to get his legs out of range, till the two of them were lurching round and round in a tight circle, the teacher grunting with effort, the boy going 'Ow, miss,' at each slap, and laughing in between.

The children loved it. Victor Hammond was the class clown, always in trouble, never worried except on the rare occasions when a teacher sent him to the Head. The Head was Mr Nicholson. *Old Nick*, the children called him, after the devil. He kept a long, springy cane in his study, and any boy unlucky enough to be sent to him was treated to two strokes, known as cuts, on each hand. After this punishment the hands curled up and couldn't be opened for the rest of the day. Even Victor didn't laugh at that.

Josh watched the undignified dance of clown and teacher with both hands over his mouth so he wouldn't be seen laughing. He preferred to stay out of trouble, but deep down he wished he was just like Victor. Victor Hammond might be the class clown, but he was the class hero as well, and Josh would have liked to be a hero too.

At morning break, admiring fans clustered around as the lad displayed the marks of his latest run-in with Miss Bowman. The teacher's handprints stood out in red on his pale skin, every finger sharply defined. 'D'you know what they remind me of?' said Josh. 'Those pictures of Stone-Age handprints on cave walls you see in encyclopaedias.' He could tell that Miss Bowman's slaps must have really hurt, and was awed, remembering the way Victor had laughed between blows.

'Those prints have lasted five thousand years,' said swot Ken Roe. 'They're the only way we know the people who made them ever existed.' He grinned. 'P'raps you should give your legs to a museum, Victor, so folk five thousand years from now'll know Miss Bowman existed.'

'They'll know,' growled Victor. 'She'll still be here. She taught my *dad*, for goodness' sake. Come *on*.' He led them in a dash towards the air-raid shelter, strictly out of bounds now the war was over. 'Last one through's a sissy.'

THREE

QUEUING

Saturday morning was damp and dull, as November mornings often are. It was porridge and toast for breakfast: nobody's favourite, but food was still rationed. Jinty would have liked a boiled egg, Josh a bacon roll, and Mum anything with a bit of flavour. She gazed through the kitchen window at the dripping garden. 'Looks like a Snakes-and-Ladders-by-the-fire day for you two,' she said, 'once you've been down for the groceries.'

Jinty pulled a face. 'We thought we'd play out, Mum, look for a bit of excitement.'

Her mother smiled wanly. '*Excitement*, love, in Coney Cley? I don't think you'll find any, unless Mr Manders has got hold of a few oranges.' Saul Manders ran the village shop, which was also the post office.

Josh snorted. 'If he *has*, there'll be a queue from here to Stowmarket, so I hope he hasn't. Don't fancy queuing an hour and a half for one orange.'

His mother shook her head. 'He won't have, Josh. I was joking. It'll just be the usual rations.'

Sister and brother got into macs and wellies and set off, Josh with a string bag crammed in his pocket, Jinty swinging Mum's basket. It was a short walk to Stowmarket Road, where the shop stood. There was a pub called the

Fox and Grapes, the police house, and a village hall that used to put on dances for the American airmen, and now housed a baby clinic on Tuesday mornings and a whist-drive on Friday evenings. That was as wild as it got in Coney Cley.

There was a queue outside the shop, but not for oranges. It was just the usual queue, caused by Manders having to clip coupons out of everybody's ration book to prove they'd had their tiny portions of butter, sugar, bacon and other scarce foods.

The two children tagged on the end and shuffled forward with everybody else. It wasn't long before there was a line of shoppers behind them as well, which made them feel better. There was a damp wind, and they were glad when they actually got inside the shop.

Mr Manders moved to and fro behind his counter, reaching down tins and packets, snipping out coupons, taking cash and giving change. He swapped remarks with the customers, mostly grumbles about rationing and the weather. It made a slow job slower, and was a test of everybody's patience.

Mrs Manders was in the shop, but she wasn't serving. She was reading from a pencilled list, fetching items to pack in a cardboard box on the floor and ticking them off. Having nothing else to do, the children watched her.

'Who's *that* stuff for, I wonder?' murmured Josh.

His sister shrugged. 'Somebody old?' she suggested. 'Or lame?'

'Or lazy,' put in Josh. 'Can't be bothered queuing. Hey!' He brightened. 'We could get Mum to put an order in every week—save us traipsing down here.'

'Sssh!' Jinty put a finger over her lips. 'Pipe down, Josh, the whole shop can hear you.' She whispered, 'There'll be a charge, you twerp. Delivery charge, and Mum's got hardly any money. Besides, it gets us out for a while, even on days like this.'

They fell silent. Manders chuntered on, his wife worked at her list. Jinty wished there were coupons in her ration book for excitement: two ounces a week would do.

10

FOUR

THE LOWEST FORM OF WIT

Back home, the pair dumped their purchases on the kitchen table. 'You were right,' Josh told their mother. 'No oranges. Can we play out now?'

Mrs Linton smiled. 'I suppose so, but goodness knows what you'll find to do on a horrible day like this, love.'

'What did *you* use to do when you were our age, Mum?' asked Jinty.

Their mother shrugged. 'Much the same things you do, Jinty. Tin Can Squat, Hide and Seek, Tig. Girls had dolls in prams, boys played with marbles or conkers. Not much different from now really, except there were bull's-eyes and aniseed balls and sherbet dabs. And we'd usually play indoors on days like today.'

Josh sighed. 'Bull's-eyes. What I wouldn't give for a bagful of those, Mum.'

'I know, love. They'll be back, I

11

expect—we don't know when, that's all. Wrap up warm now, there's a spiteful wind. Lunch is at one.'

The boy grinned. 'I hope it's stuffed cabbage again.'

'No, you *don't*,' retorted his mother. 'That's what's known as sarcasm, young man: the lowest form of wit.'

They walked chuckling down the path. 'Yesterday it was *the happiest shortfall in history*,' said Jinty, 'and today it's *the lowest form of wit*.'

'What you blithering about, Sis?' growled Josh. '*What's* the happiest shortfall in history?'

'According to Doggy, the Thousand Year Reich—which only managed twelve years.' Doggy was Jinty's class teacher. His real name was Mr Barker, and he'd been an air gunner in the war. 'Mind you,' she added, 'I don't suppose *you* know what it means, the Thousand Year Reich.'

'*Course* I do,' retorted Josh. 'It's how long the Nazis were going to rule the world.'

'Smartypants,' muttered his sister.

Shadows Lane was at the far end of the village. It wasn't much used, because it didn't lead anywhere except to Cornflower Cottage, which had stood empty for many years. Ranks of ancient elms lined both sides, their branches interlocking overhead, forming in summer the dim green tunnel that gave the lane its name. Now, the ground was carpeted with fallen leaves, and the bare branches sieved a feeble light which fell on them.

Josh shivered as the pair turned into the lane's gloomy mouth. 'The spookiness starts here,' he murmured.

Jinty snorted. 'Does it heck, it's just a lane.' She strode ahead, kicking up showers of leaves. They were damp, so that some clung to her socks and bare knees. Josh came more slowly, weaving between russet drifts.

Cornflower Cottage was on the left, half hidden beyond a hedge of wildly neglected box, three times Jinty's height. There'd once been a gateway in this hedge, with a low gate of wrought

13

iron. Somebody had salvaged the gate to be turned into a gun for the last war, or the war before that. The hedge had tried to close the gap, and had almost succeeded. Brother and sister stood gazing through the ragged slot that remained; the house was just visible through a dripping tangle of azalea and rhododendron. They saw four black windows, two upstairs and two downstairs, and a door in the middle that had once been white, with two steps leading up to it. It was like an infant's drawing of a house.

'Go on, then,' whispered Jinty.

'Where?'

'Into the garden, of course, you clot.' She looked at him. 'Not *scared*, are you?'

'Course not. I'm . . . er . . . reconnoitring.'

'Why? D'you think there could be a minefield or a machine-gun nest or something?'

Josh shook his head. 'Not a minefield or a machine-gun nest obviously, but there might be *something*.'

Jinty chuckled. 'Want me to go first, then?'

'No, I *don't*. Give me a couple of secs, that's all.'

'OK,' agreed his sister. 'One sec . . . two secs, *go*.'

She gave him a bit of a push, and Josh made a business of shoving his way through the wet, scratchy box. Jinty followed. They stood on a slimy bit of crazy paving, not sure what they'd come here to do. 'I know,' hissed Jinty. 'Let's circle the house, see what's round the back.'

Josh nodded. 'Yes, all right, come on.'

They'd just stepped off the path when Josh noticed something near his foot. Something white, half hidden under a clump of leaf mould. 'Hang on.' He bent, flicked the debris aside with his fingers and recoiled with a cry.

'What the heck's *up*?' demanded Jinty, who wasn't feeling nearly as brave as she pretended.

Josh pointed. 'Look.'

Jinty looked and saw a tooth.

A human tooth.

15

FIVE

THE LESSER-SPOTTED TOOTH WARBLER

'How the heck did that get here?' cried Jinty.

'Sssh!' Josh glanced all around. 'Pipe down, Sis, you might bring somebody.'

'*Who?* No one comes here, you know that.'

'Yes, but . . .' He nodded at the tooth. 'It didn't get here by itself, did it?'

'A bird might have dropped it.'

'What—the lesser-spotted tooth warbler? Talk sense, for goodness' sake. It came in a mouth, and the mouth was part of someone's face, and that someone was here not long ago. It wouldn't be clean and shiny like that if it'd been on the ground a while.'

Without noticing, the pair had begun backing towards the gateway. Circling the house had become a non-starter. Somewhere, not far away, was a person

16

with a gap where a tooth ought to be. He might be lurking among the rhododendrons right now, watching them. Tang of blood in his mouth, smear on his lip.

If it was a *he*.

Could be a *she*.

Or even an *it*, and that was the scariest thought of all.

Back in Shadows Lane, their eyes darted everywhere. Nothing had followed them through the hedge. Nothing stirred in the dark under the elms. All they had to do was walk up the lane, but Josh's nerve cracked. 'Run!' he yelled, and they did, casting fearful glances back.

Excitement's like chocolate cake: the first bite's delicious, but one thin slice is usually enough.

'Maybe we should've brought the tooth,' said Jinty, when the top of the lane came in sight and she was feeling brave again.

Josh shivered. 'What *for*, Sis—it was horrid.'

'Could've shown it to Mum,' she said. 'Asked her how *she* thinks it might have got there.'

Josh shook his head. 'I don't think we should tell Mum where we've been, Sis. She'll say it's dark and lonely and we ought not to go there. The Americans used to walk girls down Shadows Lane, you know, only they called it Lovers' Lane. Donnie Walker's sister was one of them. He got a set of aircraft recognition cards from a Yank she walked out with. Brings 'em to school, the big show-off.' He looked at his sister. 'D'you think we'll go down there again then, Sis?' He hoped not.

'P'raps,' said Jinty, 'but not till bull's-eyes come back.'

SIX

EUNICE

They didn't mention Shadows Lane at home, but that didn't mean they weren't thinking about it. Jinty was still thinking about it as she lay in bed that night, and when she drifted off to sleep a nightmare wrapped her in its foggy tentacles.

She was in Shadows Lane, but not with her brother. It was night, and her companion was Eunice, Donnie Walker's big sister, who'd arranged to meet an American airman. Jinty felt uncomfortable, she didn't understand why Eunice had brought her along. She said, 'Eunice, I'm too young, and anyway the Americans went home ages ago.'

'Not *this* one,' laughed Eunice, as a tall figure stepped from behind an elm. '*He* can't go till he finds his tooth.'

The man rushed up and thrust his leering face into Jinty's. There was a gap where a tooth had been and his mouth shone with blood. 'Look—it's only a *gum*, chum!' he roared, and Jinty knew it was all her fault. She screamed and screamed . . .

. . . and her screams woke her. She sat bolt upright, clutching the eiderdown, staring into the dark. The man had melted away, leaving the echo of his roar. There was no Eunice either, and this wasn't Shadows Lane.

'Jinty, what on *earth*'s the matter?' Light made her screw her eyes shut as her mother hurried into the room and took her in her arms.

'The *American*,' blurted Jinty, clinging, still tangled in shreds of dream. 'He thinks I've got his tooth.'

'Ssssh!' Her mother rocked her. 'There's no American, darling. You had a horrid dream, that's all. It's gone now, there's just you and me and your little room, and *goodness*, how you're shivering.' She sat back and looked at her daughter. 'D'you want to come in with me, love, just for tonight?'

Jinty nodded. 'Yes please, Mum.'

And she did.

SEVEN

THAT'S HOLLYWOOD

Sunday breakfast. Mum at the cooker, frying bread. Three eggs in a glass bowl, the ration for a week. Jinty, sitting at the table, breathed in, the

20

scent of hot fat bringing water to her mouth. A runny egg on a crunchy fried slice—heaven.

She'd slept soundly in Mum's bed. She hadn't forgotten her nightmare, but it seemed more daft than scary in the light of day. A roaring American, for goodness' sake, looking for his lost tooth. Barmy.

Josh walked in, pulling a Fair Isle jumper over his head. 'You slept with Mum,' he accused. 'I saw you come out of her room.'

'That'll be enough from you, young man,' warned his mother. 'Your sister had a nightmare, it can happen to anybody. Say *good morning* like a civilized person and sit down, or I just might feed your egg to the cat.'

'Morning, Mum,' mumbled Josh. 'Morning, Sis.' He stuck his tongue out at the tabby by the stove. 'Morning, Buster, hard luck.' He sat down and looked at Jinty. 'Come on, then—what happened in your nightmare?'

'Joshua,' warned his mother, flipping a slice in the pan.

'It's all right, Mum,' said Jinty with a

21

watery smile. 'I dreamed I was in Shadows Lane, Josh, with Eunice Walker. A Yank yelled at me—he'd lost a tooth.'

'Eunice *Walker*?' cried Josh. 'Why *her*, for pete's sake?'

He didn't ask why Shadows Lane, or why a tooth: he *knew* why.

Jinty shrugged. 'I don't know, Josh. It was a dream, anything can happen in a dream.' She looked him in the eye. 'Didn't *you* dream?'

'Well, I . . .' He fiddled with his cutlery. 'I never remember my dreams. I might have, but it's gone now.' He'd had a scary dream which he remembered vividly, but he wasn't going to admit it.

It was a dry morning, so once breakfast was cleared away the pair put on scarves and coats and left the house. They split up at the gate, Jinty to call for her best friend, Josh to meet his chums in the bus shelter on the Green.

'Morning, Mrs Tasker,' said Jinty when her friend's mother answered the door. 'Is Sandra coming out?'

'She is, love. Come in a minute.'

Jinty's friend appeared, wrapped up against the cold. 'Where will you go?' asked Mrs Tasker.

'I thought the park,' said Sandra. She looked at Jinty. 'If that's all right with you?'

Jinty nodded. 'It is. We can sit in the belvedere.'

The belvedere was a round wooden structure like a bandstand, with a curved bench. It had a tiled roof and open sides. Sandra's mother shivered. 'Bit chilly for that,' she said.

Sandra shook her head. 'We won't even notice, Mum, once we start chatting.'

It wasn't much of a park, especially with the café closed for winter and the swings taken in, but it was quiet. The pair had the belvedere to themselves. They huddled on the bench, and Jinty told her friend about her visit with Josh to Cornflower Cottage, and about its tangled garden and the tooth.

'A *tooth*?' gasped Sandra. 'How the heck . . .?'

'That's what *we* wondered,' said Jinty. 'I had a nightmare about it last

23

night.'

'I'm not surprised,' murmured Sandra. 'I've never been *near* the place, and I certainly won't go now you've told me *that*. Will *you* go again?'

Jinty smiled. 'I told Josh I'd go when bull's-eyes come back.'

'Well, you're welcome.' Her friend shivered. 'Anyway, my mum says Shadows Lane's got a curse on it.'

'What makes her say *that*?'

'My sister, Janet. She used to walk down Shadows Lane with Doug—you know, the Yank she married?'

Jinty nodded. 'I know. Mum says she'll be living in one of those gorgeous houses you see in films, with fridges and showers and white telephones, eating ham and eggs every day and driving around in a big posh car.'

Sandra pulled a face. 'Your mum's wrong, Jinty. Our Janet lives in a sort of shack with an outside privy and no running water. Doug's mum and grandma live there as well, and there are only three rooms. *She* pictured it like your mum, that's why she went, but that's Hollywood, not Georgia.'

'Poor thing,' breathed Jinty.

EIGHT

TWERP

Donnie Walker fanned out his pack of aircraft recognition cards like a Mississippi gambler. 'I know every one of these,' he boasted. He held them out to Josh. 'Pick one,' he invited. 'Go on: *any* one, and I'll tell you what it is.'

Josh shook his head. 'Give it a rest, Donnie, for heaven's sake. We *know* you know 'em, and nobody gives a hoot.'

'That's right,' drawled Victor Hammond, 'nobody does, so put a sock in it, you twerp.'

'D'you know what a twerp *is*?' put in Ken Roe.

'No, but I bet *you* do,' sighed Victor. He wished the class swot would stop coming to the shelter, and so did the others, but Ken had a thick skin: you could mock and insult him, and he'd just keep coming back for more.

'It's a pregnant fish,' he said.

'So're *you*,' growled Peter Garfield, the fifth member of the gang. 'That's why you're called Roe.'

This got a laugh from the others. The swot scowled, scuffing the concrete floor with his shoe. He could hardly wait for next year when he'd pass the Scholarship, move to the grammar school in Stowmarket and wave these village bumpkins goodbye. It was no fun without real friends.

He fished in his pocket and drew out a bent cigarette. 'Anyone got a match?' Cigs were scarce; he'd pinched this one from his dad's precious packet of ten to buy popularity, or at any rate acceptance.

'Yes,' chirped the class clown, 'your face and a cow's bum.' This time the laughter was subdued: all eyes were on the coveted cigarette.

'Here.' Casually, Donnie held out a Zippo lighter, which flared with the authentic clunk.

'Wow!' breathed Victor. 'Where the heck did you get *that*, Donnie?'

Donnie grinned. 'Same place I got the cards: sister's boyfriend.'

Victor chuckled. 'I hope she *married* him, mate, after all that lovely bribery.'

Donnie shrugged. 'She would have, but he got killed, last week of the war: remember?' He took the cigarette from Ken.

Josh nodded. 'I remember.' He gazed across the Green. A toddler was throwing cubes of bread to some ducks on the pond, while its mother kept a watchful eye. 'Me and Jinty were down Shadows Lane yesterday.' He spoke casually, hoping the others would be impressed by his laconic style.

Donnie took a drag on the cigarette and passed it on to Peter Garfield. 'Were you?' he asked, smoke rolling out of his mouth. 'Why?'

Josh shrugged. 'Collecting our excitement ration.'

'And did you find it?'

'Sort of.'

'What d'you mean, *sort of*?' demanded Victor. 'Did you get as far as the haunted house, see the ghost?'

'We got as far as the garden, found a

tooth.'

'A *tooth*?' The clown scowled. 'What, a horse's tooth, a dog's, or was it out of a comb?'

'It was human.'

'Ah. And was that as exciting as it got?'

'It . . . spooked us, we didn't hang about.'

'You *should* have,' said Peter, taking a second drag on Ken's ciggy.

'Hey!' squawked the swot. 'That's not fair, it's *my* turn, pass it on.'

Peter let him have it, blowing smoke in his face as he did so. He looked at Josh. 'It could have been the start of an adventure, you dunce. Hey!' He glanced round the group. 'Why don't we go there now, all of us, and investigate? There might have been a murder.'

Ken Roe shook his head. 'I can't, I've got church with my mum and dad at eleven.'

Peter shrugged. 'Nobody asked you, Swot. The rest of us?'

Donnie and Victor nodded, stood up. Josh wasn't keen, but he didn't want his chums to know that. He got up with them. Without a word, the provider of smokes handed what was left of the cigarette to Josh and walked off, dejected. His classmates left the shelter and set off for Shadows Lane.

NINE

SPRING

The four boys stood among fallen leaves, peering through the gap in the wild hedge. Donnie nudged Josh. 'Where's this famous tooth then, Linton?'

'Through here,' murmured Josh. 'On the left.'

'Well, what're we waiting for? Show us.'

They followed him through the scratchy gap. It wasn't as scary now the gang was here. Josh advanced the few steps he'd taken yesterday, peering at the ground, but there was no sign of the tooth.

'It seems to have gone,' he muttered. 'I'm *sure* this was the spot.'

'Crumbs,' whispered Victor. '*The Walking Tooth of Shadows Lane*, episode two.'

'Not funny, Victor,' murmured Josh. 'I tell you, it was *here*: someone must have taken it.'

Peter chuckled. 'That'll be the Tooth Fairy, then.'

Josh turned on his companions, his cheeks flushed. 'All right, you lot, that'll do. Who cares about some old tooth, anyway? We've come for a bit of excitement. Jinty and I meant to circle the cottage, see what it's like round the back. Why don't we do that, instead of standing here giggling like a pack of Brownies?'

'OK, Brown Owl.' Victor smiled. 'Lead on.'

Josh pushed into a jungle of rhododendron ten feet high. The others followed in single file. The evergreen foliage was so dense it screened out all sunlight: nothing could grow in its shadow. Underfoot was a thick carpet of musty leaf mould, layer

30

upon layer. One side of the cottage was visible on the right, about twenty yards away. They kept wary eyes on it as they progressed, but there was no door: no spook was about to burst out screeching and run at them. There was a small round window like a porthole downstairs, and a narrow rectangular one directly above it upstairs. The boys paused to gaze at these but saw only blackness, and moved on.

'Oh *crikey*, what's *that*?' groaned Victor as the back of the house came in sight. The others froze, looking where his finger pointed. The rhododendron had thinned, giving way to a stretch of mossy lawn. In the middle, a girl in historical dress was looking straight at them.

'It's the *ghost*!' croaked Donnie. 'I'm off.' He turned and crashed into the jungle. Peter stumbled after him. Josh was about to run too, when Victor let out a delighted whoop.

'It's a *statue*, you duffers!' he crowed. 'I *knew* it was, why didn't *you*?'

Josh tried to look like somebody who hadn't been about to run, though he

31

was ashen-faced and shaking. '*Course* it's a statue,' he murmured. 'I knew as soon as I saw it.' He yelled after Donnie and Peter. 'Come back, you heroes, it's just a block of stone.'

'I knew all the time,' lied Peter as he crept back looking sheepish. 'I was just kidding.'

'So was I,' claimed Donnie. 'In fact, my sister told me there was a statue. She came in here once with her boyfriend and saw it.'

It was lies, all of it. Only Victor had realized that the figure was a statue, and even *he*'d suffered a brief jolt before he realized. Nobody felt like talking about it, though they'd laugh later on. Nobody's as brave as they pretend to be, in war or peace.

The back of Cornflower Cottage was very like the front. Two windows upstairs, two downstairs, and a door in the middle. The four stood beside the statue, whose name turned out to be 'Spring', each wondering whether he dared suggest going closer, even knocking on the door. As they lingered, undecided, something moved at an upstairs window. Four pairs of eyes swung to the shadowed glass, fastened on it, and transmitted the same horrifying message.

A skull . . .

TEN

CHASED UP A LADDER

'What on earth have you been *doing*, Joshua?' asked his mother as he came into the house. 'There are twigs in your stockings and a dead leaf in your hair. You look like somebody who's slept in the woods.'

'Oh, well . . . we were playing at kicking up leaves, Mum.'

'Kicking up *leaves*?' She sighed. 'D'you think you might start to grow up someday, love?' She studied his face. 'You look a bit pale: nothing's happened, has it?'

'*Happened*—what could have happened, Mum? We were playing, that's all.'

'That's good, then.' His mother smiled. 'Brush that stuff off yourself outside, then go and wash your hands for lunch. It's shepherd's pie.'

He met Jinty at the top of the stairs. She grabbed his arm. 'What've you *really* been up to?' she demanded. 'I heard Mum asking you stuff.' She frowned. 'You may be able to fool her, but you can't fool me.'

'Ssssh!' Josh pressed a finger to his lips. 'If you can hear from up here, so can Mum from down there. We were in Shadows Lane and I've got to talk to you, but not now. See you in a minute.'

There wasn't much shepherd in the pie. Shepherd was what Josh called the layer of mince at the bottom of the dish, underneath the mashed potato. It was a thin layer, because the meat ration was meagre. The tastiest part was the crust of mousetrap cheese on top.

'How was *your* morning, love?' asked Mum, spooning pie onto Jinty's plate. 'Did you call for Sandra?'

Jinty nodded. 'Yes, we went to the park.'

Her mother shivered. 'I hope you ran about, kept yourselves warm.'

'No, Mum, we just talked. In the belvedere.'

'Good grief, it's a wonder you didn't die of exposure. Was anybody else there?'

Jinty shook her head. 'Not a soul.' She was staring at her brother, but he kept his head down, making patterns in the mash with his fork.

When the lunch things were cleared away, Mum set off to phone Grandma from the box in the village, as she did every Sunday. It was her ambition to have a phone installed at home, but the little she earned doing repairs and alterations to neighbours' clothes wouldn't run to it.

'Right,' said Jinty, as the door closed behind their mother, 'what happened in Shadows Lane, Josh?'

Josh pulled a face. 'It wasn't the lane, exactly, it was the cottage. There *is* a ghost, Sis, and it's got to be a skeleton.'

'You mean, you actually *saw* this ghost, Josh?' Jinty looked sceptical.

The boy nodded. 'As plain as I see you now, I swear.'

'Where was it?'

'A skull, looking out of an upstairs window, round the back.'

'Windows reflect things. Are you sure it wasn't a reflection you saw—a branch swaying in the breeze, something like that?'

Josh shook his head. 'It was *nothing* like that. I wish it was. Victor Hammond saw it too, *and* Donnie Walker and Peter Garfield. Ask 'em at school tomorrow if you don't believe me.'

Jinty nodded. 'Don't worry, I will, and perhaps we could all go together next Saturday and have another look.'

Josh shook his head. 'Not *me*. You said you weren't off down Shadows Lane again till bull's-eyes come back. And I've seen as much of Boney as I ever want to see.'

Jinty looked at him. 'Boney?'

'Yes, Victor christened him Boney. If it *is* a he. Might be a girl skeleton: a walled-up nun or something.'

'Well,' said his sister, 'that's for us to

find out, isn't it? More exciting than Snakes and Ladders.'

'Oh, I don't know.' Josh grinned. 'Have you never been chased up a ladder by an adder, Sis? Now *there's* a nightmare waiting to happen.'

ELEVEN

BEAUTIFUL BLONDE

Class Sevens don't talk to kids in Class Six. They're just kids. Jinty was keen to check out her brother's unlikely tale, but she had to shake off Sandra Tasker and wait till nobody was looking before approaching Victor Hammond.

She sidled up to him. 'I want to talk to you,' she murmured. 'Somewhere private.'

He was playing conkers with Peter Garfield. 'Shelter,' he told her, 'after this game.' He swung his conker at Peter's.

Jinty tutted and walked on with her nose in the air.

In the forbidden air-raid shelter, two Class Fives were sharing a cigarette. 'Shove off,' snarled Jinty. '*Now*. And leave the ciggy.' She never smoked, but Victor Hammond did.

He came, bringing Peter Garfield with him. That was OK, Peter had been at the cottage too. 'Present for you,' she said, handing the cigarette to Victor.

'Ooh, *ta*.' He sounded surprised. 'What d'you want, Jinty?'

She looked at him. 'You went down to Cornflower Cottage yesterday with my brother, is that right?'

Victor nodded, taking a drag on the cigarette. ' 'S right. What of it?'

'He reckons he saw a ghost at one of the windows.'

'*Does* he?' He blew out a plume of smoke. 'We agree not to tell anyone, so the twerp goes and blabs to his big sister.' He looked at her. 'Yes, he saw a ghost. So did I.'

'We *all* did,' put in Peter. 'It was a skeleton.'

Jinty smiled in the dark. 'Know what *I* bet?'

'What?'

'I bet you made the whole thing up. You didn't find anything exciting, so you invented something.'

Victor passed the cigarette to Peter and shook his head. 'You couldn't be more wrong, Jinty. We saw it all right, and I for one wouldn't go in that garden again if you paid me.'

'Me neither,' said Peter. 'It was horrible. I'd rather have two on each hand from Old Nick than see Boney again.' He looked at her. '*You* go,' he challenged. 'You'll soon find out if we made it up or not.'

Jinty nodded. 'I might just do that.' She walked towards the light. 'See you later, boys.' She hoped she sounded like a beautiful blonde in a gangster film.

TWELVE

OXYMORON

Walking home, Josh said, 'You got me in hot water with my chums, Jinty. I wasn't supposed to tell anybody about . . . you know . . . the cottage.'

His sister shrugged. 'You *said* ask them. How was I supposed to do that without mentioning it, you dope?'

'So, do you believe me now?'

Jinty pulled a face. 'I don't want to, but Victor and Peter are scared stiff, I can tell they aren't pretending.' She looked at her brother. 'I want to see Boney for myself, Josh, and I want you to come with me.'

Josh shook his head. 'You said, *not till bull's-eyes come back*, and I say the same.'

'You're scared.'

'Yes, I am. *You* were scared last Saturday, and you only saw a tooth.'

'Good day at school, you two?' Mum greeted them when they got home.

Jinty frowned. 'The words *good day* and *school* don't belong together, Mum. They're what old Doggy calls an oxymoron—like the words *ooh, delicious* and *sago pudding.*'

Her mother smiled. 'I don't remember being taught about oxymorons when *I* was at school, Jinty. I remember a few *morons*, but that's another matter. As for sago pudding, lots of people in Europe would say "Ooh, delicious" to a bowl, if only they could get it.'

Jinty made no reply. She knew which people Mum was talking about. There'd been a picture in the paper once, a couple of years back. Stick-thin folk in striped pyjamas, with shaven heads and haunted eyes. You couldn't tell which were women and which were men. She'd held up the paper and asked, 'Mum, who are these peop—?'

Her mother had snatched the paper out of her hands before she could finish her question. 'Never mind, love,' she'd murmured. 'It's not for little girls.'

She'd found out, though. Overheard

41

two women in a queue at Manders',
talking about the same picture. The
thin folk were prisoners in a
concentration camp. Belsen. Those
in the picture were survivors, but
thousands of others had starved, or
died of horrible diseases. The boss of
the camp was in prison—both women
said he should be hanged and he had
been, just a few weeks ago. That had
been in the paper too.

'It's not sago pudding *today*, I hope,'
growled Josh, shrugging off his coat.

'No, Joshua, it isn't,' said Mum. 'It's
that good old standby, semolina with
prunes.'

Brother and sister bent over and
gagged, clutching their throats.

THIRTEEN

WOOF

All that week, Jinty kept pestering her
brother to go with her to Cornflower
Cottage. The tale she'd heard from

Victor and Peter haunted her imagination. It sounded like something in a story by M. R. James, not something you'd actually see in an ordinary place like Coney Cley.

It was almost December, too dark to go anywhere after school. She hoped that by Friday, Josh might relent and agree to one more expedition.

He didn't, which was why she was still pestering him in Manders' queue on Saturday morning.

'Five minutes, that's all,' she nagged. 'Just enough time to get round the back and look up at that window. If there's nothing there, I promise I'll still believe you, and I won't ask to go again.'

Josh shook his head. There was a paper sack of dog biscuits on the floor. A few biscuits had escaped through a tear in the sack. He slid one towards himself with the side of his shoe, picked it up while Saul Manders wasn't looking and proceeded to nibble it.

Jinty pulled a disgusted face. 'If you won't come to the cottage, I'll tell Mum you've been eating dog biscuits.'

'Woof!' barked Josh. 'What d'you

think'd happen if I told her you've been nagging me to go down Shadows Lane? You *know* she doesn't like us going there.'

Jinty was about to reply when Mrs Manders spoke through the grille of the post-office counter. They hadn't noticed her behind the mesh. 'Stay *right* away from Shadows Lane, the pair of you,' she warned. 'There's nothing there that's any of your business, and that goes for your chums as well. If I see children snooping around Shadows Lane, it'll be *me* telling tales to parents.' She looked at Josh. 'And if I catch you pinching my biscuits again I'll add them to your mother's bill, and she wouldn't like *that*, would she?'

'How did *I* know they were her biscuits,' said Josh when they got outside. 'I thought they were for dogs.'

'Idiot,' spluttered Jinty, laughing in spite of herself.

Josh frowned. 'It's a bit steep, though, isn't it, Sis? I mean, what's it to *her* if we go down Shadows Lane? Does she *own* it or something? Bad enough Mum and the teachers always telling us what to do and what not to do, without the grocer's missus joining in.'

Jinty saw an opportunity. 'You're absolutely *right*, Josh,' she said. 'What right has Mrs Manders to tell us where we can or can't go? It's a free country, and that's what we're all supposed to have been fighting for, isn't it: to keep the country free? So, I vote we go down there *today*: the minute we get rid of these groceries.'

'Yes,' growled Josh. 'That's *exactly* what we'll do.' He grinned. '*That*'ll teach her to gurn at us through her rotten little grille like a chimp at the zoo.'

FOURTEEN

FOUR SLICES OF SPAM

Paul Bluet shivered, holding his hands near the ancient stove, rubbing them together. It wasn't really cold, not like in Poland, but he felt it badly enough to need an overcoat indoors. Four slices of

Spam spat in an iron pan on the hotplate. They filled the kitchen with an aroma that made Paul's mouth water and his stomach yearn. It was as much as he could do to keep from scooping the meat onto a plate half done, yet when at length he sat down with the meal in front of him, he couldn't eat. He gazed at the cooling slices as though he didn't believe they were really there, while taking occasional sips of cold water from his glass.

It was the others. They weren't here— they were dead, behind distant wire—but he felt them every time he tried to eat. Their hungry eyes, their cramped guts, their question: always the same bewildered question. Why you? Why you with all this food?

Paul had no answer. He didn't know why he'd survived and they had not. He'd been no better than them. No worse and no better. He'd tried over and over to tell himself it wasn't his fault, it was the luck of the draw, but still it was a struggle to eat anything, and to keep from throwing up on the rare occasions when he did. See this food? *the voice in his head would murmur.* Just what's here on your plate? Well, this might have been enough to keep four of you alive till the Russians came. It might easily have been enough, and yet you're about to stuff it all into your greedy belly at one go. I don't know how you can bear to live with yourself.

The slices were quite cold now, in a puddle of congealed fat. Slowly Paul picked up his knife and fork, cut off a tiny pink triangle and speared it on the fork. As the morsel neared his lips he tried to see crystal waters falling over mossy stones into a clear pool, but instead a picture came to him of a corpse he'd seen near the camp crematorium. A piece of flesh had been bitten out of one withered thigh by some desperate inmate: a piece about the size of this one.

With a harsh cry of revulsion, Paul flung away his cutlery and staggered heaving towards the sink.

FIFTEEN

MAIRZY DOATS

The fallen leaves were black and slimy now, it was no fun kicking them about, and Josh was feeling grumpy anyway. His sister had taken advantage of his indignation at Mrs Manders to get him here. She'd tricked him, the way girls do, and so here they were in Shadows Lane, where he thought he'd never be again.

He was scared. That skeletal thing at the upstairs window was real. He'd seen it move. It was horrible. It was all right for Jinty, she didn't believe in Boney, she thought he'd made him up. *Look* at her, marching along with her nose in the air, whistling *Mairzy Doats*. She'd whistle a different tune if she saw what he'd seen.

'Come on, Josh, you're *loitering*.' She waited for him to catch up. 'Who scares you most, eh—Boney, or Mrs Manders?'

48

'Not scared of Mrs Manders,' he growled. 'Silly old trout.'

His sister grinned. 'Boney, then.'

He shook his head. 'Not scared of *anything.*'

'Doesn't look like it.' She started to sing loudly:
'Mairzy doats and dozy doats
And liddle lamzy divey,
A kiddley divey too,
Wouldn't you?'

The sudden noise startled a blackbird, which exploded from an elm thicket, making Josh jump.

'Put a sock in it, Sis, for pete's sake,' he snapped. 'It's spooky enough without *you* bellowing gibberish.'

'Tisn't gibberish,' shot back Jinty. 'Listen:
Mares eat oats and does eat oats
And little lambs eat ivy,
A kid'll eat—'

'Yeah yeah yeah, I *know. Everybody* knows, so keep quiet or I'm off home.'

He went first into the garden, because he'd said he wasn't scared. It was soggy underfoot. They stood in the gateway, gazing towards the cottage.

Everything looked the same as before.

'Go on, then,' hissed Jinty.

'I am,' murmured Josh. 'It's this way.' He stepped off the bit of paving, tracking left, forcing himself not to glance down where the tooth had been. Jinty followed, telling herself it was all rubbish, there are no such things as ghosts.

They tiptoed through the rhododendron jungle. Josh kept a wary eye on the round window in the side of the house, and the slim one upstairs, seeing only blackness. Where the jungle thinned, he paused.

'In a minute you'll see a girl,' he whispered, 'but it's just a statue. We were standing by it when we saw . . .' He shivered, fighting an urge to run.

Jinty nodded. 'Lead on. I won't scream, promise.'

His scalp crawled as they emerged onto the mossy lawn. There were four windows they might be seen from, if eyeless sockets can see. And that door could fly open at any second.

They stood by the statue. 'She's called Spring,' murmured Jinty.

Josh nodded, staring at the upstairs window. His whole attention was on it, he hadn't heard what she said.

It was blank. Nothing looked back at him. A part of him regretted this—he'd wanted his sister as scared as he'd been. But mostly he was relieved. He *willed* the apparition to stay hidden. A few seconds more, to prove he wasn't afraid, then they could turn and go back. He yearned to be on the far side of that gap in the hedge. It was all he asked. He wouldn't care if Jinty didn't believe him, just as long as he need never come here again.

Seconds passed. The windows stayed blank, the door stayed shut.

'Where's old Boney, then?' mocked Jinty, breaking the spell.

Josh shook his head. 'Who cares? Come on.' He turned to recross the lawn, and froze.

Among the rhododendrons the skeleton stood, watching.

51

SIXTEEN

WHAT WILL IT DO TO US?

Jinty didn't scream, but she whimpered, grabbing her brother's sleeve. 'Wh . . . what *is* it?' she croaked. 'What will it do to us?'

Josh shook his head. He didn't dare take his eyes off the hideous figure. 'That's Boney,' he said huskily, 'and I don't *know* what he'll do.'

'P'raps if we start to go, he'll let us . . .'

The boy nodded. 'Not back, though, we're cut off. Round the house, then run for the gap and hope he's not there first. Ready?'

'Yes.'

'*Go!*'

They pelted across the spongy turf, sobbing. Both yearned to glance back, but daren't. How fast do apparitions move? Can you flee from them, or do they go wherever they want to in a flash? *Was Boney already guarding the*

52

gap?

The lawn ended. They swerved right, racing down the side of the cottage, scattering canes and strings over what had once been a kitchen garden.

Another swerve and they were at the front, crashing through rhododendrons, angling towards the hedge. As the unguarded gap came in sight, Jinty risked a look behind. Except for branches they'd swept aside, nothing moved in the shadows. They hit the gap and burst through in a shower of sprigs, like horses at Becher's Brook.

They didn't dare stop, but reeled gasping up the lane till shortage of breath felled Josh, who collapsed on a carpet of dead leaves. Jinty sank panting to her knees beside him, looking back. No apparition had followed them through the hedge. The only skeletons were leafless elms, whose fingers clawed the sky.

SEVENTEEN

OILING THE BIKE

The police house stood close to the Manders' shop. When the shop closed at midday for the weekend, Ruth Manders walked the few yards that separated the buildings and rang the doorbell under the blue lamp. The policeman's wife opened the door.

'Good afternoon, Mrs Manders. Is it Norbert you're wanting?' Norbert Lassiter was the village bobby, and Coney Cley's only policeman.

Ruth Manders nodded. 'Yes please, if you're not in the middle of lunch.'

The younger woman shook her head. 'We don't eat till half-past. Come on in.' She led Ruth along the hallway to the living room, which doubled as a police station. 'Have a seat and I'll call him: he's pottering about in the shed.'

Ruth lowered herself into an easy chair. After a minute the bobby appeared, wiping his hands on a rag.

54

He gave her a rueful smile. 'Sorry, Mrs Manders, I was oiling the bike. Nothing's the matter, I hope?'

Ruth shook her head. 'Nothing drastic, Mr Lassiter. It's just that some of the children seem suddenly to have started taking an interest in Shadows Lane. I overheard the Linton girl this morning in the shop, talking to her brother. She said, *If you won't come to the cottage, I'll tell Mum* . . . something or other. She meant Cornflower Cottage.'

The policeman nodded. 'I see. Well, it isn't so surprising, is it? I mean, youngsters always *used* to be interested in the place: reckoned it was haunted. The war gave 'em something else to think about, but now it's over they're looking for excitement, as kids do.'

Ruth Manders looked at him. 'I understand all that, Mr Lassiter, and I know Shadows Lane is the King's highway, not somebody's private road. But you and I both know that it conceals a secret just now, and that it isn't in anybody's best interest for that secret to be revealed. You know what the newspapers are like: one hint of a mystery and there'll be reporters swarming all over Coney Cley like the rats of Hamelin.'

The bobby nodded. 'You're right of course, Mrs Manders. Leave it with me, will you? I'll talk to Nicholson at the school, and perhaps the vicar, only we need to tread softly. If we make it obvious something's being hidden, the kids'll be even more interested.'

EIGHTEEN

BEANO-READING BUMPKINS

'Hey, Peter, come here a minute.'
   'What?'
   'You'll never guess who *I* saw on Saturday.'
   'Uh—King George, was it?'
   'Besides him.'
   'I give up.'
   'Boney, *outside*.'
   '*Where* outside? You didn't go to the *cottage* again?'

'I did.'

'By yourself?'

'No, me and my sister. We were by that statue, and Boney sneaked up on us through the bushes. He was about ten yards away.'

'Crikey. What did you *do*?'

'What d'you *think* we did, you twerp? We *ran*.'

It was Monday morning, before the bell. By playtime Victor Hammond knew, and Donnie Walker, and Ken Roe. The five gathered by the air-raid shelter.

'Can't be a ghost,' said Ken flatly.

The others looked irritated. 'Why not, Swot?' growled Victor.

'Ghosts haunt one spot, where something terrible happened to them when they were alive. They don't go *looking* for the ghost-hunters, the ghost-hunters have to go to *them*. *Everybody* knows that.'

Victor shook his head. 'I didn't.'

'Neither did I.'

'Me neither.'

'Nor me.'

The swot smiled. 'That's 'cause

you're *Beano*-reading bumpkins. *We've* got the *Encyclopaedia Britannica* at home, the full set.'

'I've got teeth in my gob,' said Victor. 'The full set, which is more than you'll have in a minute if you don't stop showing off.'

'So, Ken,' asked Josh, who felt Victor was too hard on the swot sometimes, 'if Boney's not a *ghost*, what the heck *is* he?'

The swot shrugged. 'I dunno, *I* haven't seen him.'

'D'you *want* to?'

Ken shook his head. 'I didn't say that.'

'Rather look him up in the "Cycle Rule Britannia", wouldn't you, Swot?' sneered Victor. 'Scared stiff, I bet.'

'No, I'm not, and I'll prove it. If you chaps're off down Shadows Lane again, let me know. I'll come with you, and I'll be first into the garden.'

Victor stuck his face into the swot's. 'You're *on*,' he hissed.

NINETEEN

A ROAD TO NOWHERE

'Hrrrmph! Good morning, boys and girls.' Old Nick gazed sternly down at the assembled pupils.

'Good morning, Mr Nicholson. Good morning, friends,' chorused one hundred and eighty voices. It was nine o'clock on Tuesday morning. Outside, a blustery wind blew sprays of rain which rattled on high windows. Not a particularly good morning, but one to cause no surprise in early December.

'I have two things to say to you all before we sing our hymn.' He scowled at somebody fidgeting near the back of the hall. '*How* many things do I have to say to you all, Victor Hammond?'

'Uh . . . three, sir, was it?'

'No, laddie, it was *not*. Tell him, Sandra Tasker.'

'Sir, two, sir.'

'Thank you, Sandra. Did you *hear* that, Victor Hammond?'

'Yes, sir.'

'Splendid. First, the air-raid shelter in the yard. Every one of you knows perfectly well that the shelter is out of bounds, yet every day teachers are having to punish pupils for breaking the rule. I've said it many times, and I'll say it once more: the war is over, so there is no need for anybody to be inside the air-raid shelter. It is *not* a Wendy house, it is *not* a club for the smokers' union, and it is *certainly* not an extra lavatory for your exclusive use, Dennis Colton. In due course, I expect the Council will get around to demolishing it, but until then we will *all* stay away from it. Won't we, Victor Hammond?'

'Yes, sir.'

'Good. The second thing I have to say is also about children going where they ought not to, but this one is even more serious. It has been reported to me that certain pupils have been trespassing on private property at the bottom of Shadows Lane.'

Josh glanced at Peter, who nudged Donnie, who pulled a face at Victor, who scowled at Ken the swot.

The Head failed to notice, and continued: 'Besides being an offence, trespass can cause distress to innocent persons. It may also be dangerous. Pupils of this school never behave in such a way as to cause distress to others, nor are they encouraged to put themselves in danger. Shadows Lane is a road to nowhere, with trees and turnip fields on either side and nothing at the end except a dilapidated cottage, of no possible interest to anyone.' His eyes swept across one hundred and eighty upturned faces. 'Stay away from Shadows Lane, and take it from me: there is no such thing as a haunted house. We will now sing hymn number forty-four: O Worship The King.'

TWENTY

PEACH

It was still raining at playtime. Pupils crammed into the covered area like matches in a box, but its roof wasn't wide enough to shelter one hundred and eighty boisterous children. Only one game was possible in the circumstances: *Drown the Duffers*. In this game, the meek and the small were jostled to the fringes of the crush, then shoved bodily out into the open. Any duffer bold enough to try getting back under cover suffered the penalty of being held, for a count of ten, under a deluge that fell through a crack in the guttering. With clothes still rationed, the school carried no spares, so victims steamed for the rest of the day in puddles, after being yelled at for being too stupid to come in out of the rain.

'Blow this for a game of soldiers,' snarled Victor, after five minutes of pushing and shoving. 'Why fight for a square foot of floor in here when there's a shelter over there doing nothing?'

'You heard Old Nick,' said Josh. '*Nobody's* allowed in the air-raid shelter.'

'Tisn't an *air-raid* shelter any more, though, is it? It's just a shelter, and we need shelter from this rain. Come *on*.'

The class clown pulled his jacket up over his head and pelted across the swirling yard. Josh followed reluctantly, hoping no teacher was watching through the staffroom window. In the shelter's gloom he bent his head and mopped his hair with his hanky, trying not to remember how it felt that time when Old Nick's cane cracked across his palm. Two of those on each hand is a lifetime's supply, thank you very much.

Victor looked at him. 'Swotty Roe peached, you know.'

'How d'you mean, peached? What about?'

'Shadows Lane, of course. How else would Nick know we'd been down there? Ken Roe's the only one who knew, and didn't go himself.'

Josh shook his head. 'He wouldn't peach, Victor. I know he's a twerp, but he'd never stoop that low. In fact, he said he'd go with us next time, didn't he, and lead the way?'

The clown laughed. 'Yes, because he knew there wasn't going to *be* a next time: he'd blabbed to the Head and Old Nick would put the place out of bounds.'

'We can't prove it.'

'No, we can't. What we *can* do is hold him to his promise.'

'We can't do that either, with Shadows Lane out of bounds.'

Victor tousled the other boy's damp hair. 'This *shelter*'s out of bounds, you ninny, but we're *here*.' He grinned. 'Out of bounds is for shirkers and duffers. Who's going to know if a bunch of us goes down there at the weekend? Old Nick won't post a sentry, will he? And he can't keep watch himself—he lives way out on the far side of Stowmarket.'

'Other people might be keeping their eyes open, such as the police.'

Victor laughed. 'The police is Norbert Lassiter, Josh. One chap for the whole village. Anyway, even if he *is* watching Shadows Lane, we can cross a turnip field and come out halfway down.' He grinned. 'I'm going to tell Roe he's leading our expedition on Saturday. He'll be in a blue funk all week.'

Josh shook his head. 'You're a devil-may-care funster, Victor, but I think we'd better get out of here before a teacher comes out with the bell.'

The bell rang before he'd finished speaking.

TWENTY-ONE

NOTHING OF A JOB

'Come.'

Reluctantly, Josh and Victor entered the Head's study. Old Nick was seated behind an oak desk strewn with papers. He looked up. 'Well?'

'Sir,' quavered Josh. 'Mr Barker sent us. He saw us coming out of the air-raid shelter.'

'Oh.' The man's bushy eyebrows rose. 'There *was* a raid, was there, at playtime?'

'N . . . no, sir.'

'Oh—I thought there must have been. Why else would you have gone into the shelter, after all I said in assembly?'

'We just, er . . .'

'The covered area's not big enough, sir,' said Victor boldly. 'It was bucketing down, kids were getting soaked. The shelter's rainproof and it wasn't doing anything, so me and Linton used it, sir, that's all. It was my idea.'

'Hmmm.' Mr Nicholson was fiddling with his smelly old pipe, filling its bowl with shreds of tobacco, tamping it down with a finger. Without looking up he said, 'I hadn't realized they'd appointed you Director of Education, Hammond. Congratulations.'

'They haven't, sir, only I just thought—'

'You decided that using the shelter as an overflow covered area for wet playtimes is a better idea than knocking it down, is that it?'

The clown nodded. 'I suppose so, sir, yes.'

The Head was silent, loading his pipe. Both boys fidgeted on the threadbare carpet, waiting. Waiting was the worst part: Josh wished he'd get up and reach for the cane, get it over with.

It felt like hours before the Head was satisfied with his pipe and laid it aside. *This is it*, thought Josh. *Two on each hand. Be brave, like Dad.*

Old Nick gazed up at Victor. 'And who's to say you're not right, laddie, eh?'

Victor goggled. '*Pardon*, sir?'

'About the shelter. It's basically sound, but it's dark inside because there are no windows. Knock out a few bricks here and there, fit some frames, nothing of a job. Certainly cheaper than extending the covered area. Yes.' He stood up. 'I'll get on to the planning department, put it to them.' He beamed at the two boys. 'Run along now,' he said. 'Don't want to be late for your next class, eh?'

TWENTY-TWO

PATAGONIA

Miss Bowman was drawing a map of Africa on the board. Donnie leaned towards Josh and hissed, 'How *many*, Josh?'

'How many *what*?'

'*Cuts*, you imbecile.'

'None.'

'What—you mean he let you *off*?'

'Yes.'

'Victor as well?'

'Yes.' Josh grinned. 'You should've seen him, he was a hero. Told Nick the covered area's too small.'

'It is, but Nick let him get away with *telling* him?'

'Better than that. He's getting on to the Council about having the shelter converted.'

'You jest.'

'No, he *said* so.'

'Wow!'

'Donald Walker.' Miss Bowman spun

round and flung her stick of chalk at Donnie. 'I don't suppose you're chattering about David Livingstone's missionary work among African natives, are you?'

'N . . . no, miss.' Donnie rubbed his forehead where the chalk had bounced off.

'I thought not. Pick up that chalk, come out here and draw Lake Victoria on the map for us.'

Donnie stood with the chalk in his hand, staring at the blackboard.

The teacher sighed. 'We're all waiting, Donald.'

'Yes, miss.' He sketched a wonky oval on the map.

Miss Bowman tutted. 'D'you think Lake Victoria's *really* in the middle of the Sahara Desert, Donald?'

'No, miss.' The class tittered.

'No, because then it wouldn't actually *be* a desert, would it?'

'No, miss.'

'No, miss.' The teacher shook her head. 'Go and sit down, Donald. It's a good job *you* weren't David Livingstone, or you'd probably have gone looking for the source of the Nile in Patagonia.'

*   *   *

Lunch time, the four boys stood at the gateway, looking across Glebe Lane at St Hilda's Church. Another week or so and they'd be over there most days, practising for the Christmas concert.

'Always freezing in that place,' grumbled Victor.

'Tell Old Nick.' Peter grinned. 'Maybe you can get him to convert the shelter into a rehearsal room.'

The clown shook his head. 'Your turn, chum. I've pushed my luck as far as it'll go.'

'It's a miracle you're not nursing raw palms,' said Ken Roe, who had joined them.

Victor glowered at him. 'It's a miracle you're not nursing black eyes, Swot, peaching on us like that.'

'Like *what*?' protested Ken. 'I never peached. I don't know what you're talking about.'

'Shadows Lane,' grated the clown.

'You must've told Old Nick we went down there: nobody else knew.'

Ken shook his head. 'I didn't tell *anybody*. Didn't I say I'd come along next time, be first into the garden?'

'Ah, yes,' crooned Victor. 'So you did: thanks for reminding me.'

'Only we *can't* now, can we?' Ken tried to look disappointed. 'Not now the Head's mentioned it.'

'Oh, don't worry about *that*,' said Victor. 'The Head and me are great chums, we plan stuff together. Conversions, things like that. No, we'll be following you down there Saturday, my old swot-box, no danger. Looking forward to it, aren't we, lads?'

TWENTY-THREE

WOLVES IN WOLVES' CLOTHING

'*Now*, boys and girls,' beamed Miss Bowman on Friday morning, 'two weeks today we'll present our Christmas concert at St Hilda's as

71

usual, but this year my class will be doing something a bit different. I've written a short play, based on the story of the Nativity, but concentrating on the shepherds, their flocks and the perils they encounter.' She smiled, her eyes panning along the rows of faces. 'In every group of people there are sheep and there are wolves. There may be shepherds too, but sadly these are rare. Hands up if you think you're a shepherd.'

Victor Hammond's hand shot up. The teacher looked at him. 'Why d'you think so, Victor?'

' 'Cause people follow me, miss.'

'Yes, they *do*, don't they, I've noticed that. Trouble is, Victor, you lead them straight into trouble. If you were a shepherd you'd steer your flock over a cliff-edge, or into a bottomless bog.' She shook her head. 'No, I see you more as wolf material really. Anyone else?' She glanced around, saw another raised hand and chuckled. '*You*, Donald Walker? *You'd* lead your thirsty sheep into the Sahara looking for Lake Victoria. Another wolf, I think.'

There were thirty-three pupils in Miss Bowman's class. In the next fifteen minutes, she assigned roles to each of them according to her whim till there were twenty-one sheep, four wolves, seven shepherds and an angel. The clown raised his hand.

'Yes, Victor?'

'Miss, there were only three shepherds.'

'*Were* there? The Bible doesn't say so. The only gospel that mentions shepherds is Luke's, and he doesn't say how many.'

'Yes, but in the Nativity play—'

'The play usually has three shepherds, but nobody knows why. It's a custom, and we're breaking it.'

'Miss?'

'What is it, Kenneth?'

'You've got Elaine Savage as the angel, miss, but all angels are men.'

'How d'you *know* that, Kenneth?'

'There's a list of them in a book of my dad's, miss. They all have boys' names—Michael, Galadriel, Gabriel and so on. There's no Sandras or Elaines.'

'Well then, Kenneth,' sighed the teacher, 'bang goes another custom.'

At break the weather was dry. There was plenty of room in the covered area. Victor's gang grabbed a corner. 'Have you noticed she's picked us *all* as wolves?' chuckled the clown.

Josh nodded. '*Course* we've noticed. She's done it on purpose, 'cause she knows we're a pack. *Hey.*' He grinned. 'There's a good echo under this roof—why don't we practise our howling?'

'Good job we're not sheep,' murmured Peter. 'I'd feel an absolute chump perfecting my bleat.'

TWENTY-FOUR

A COW'S THROAT

At half-past ten on Saturday morning, Josh and Jinty approached the bus shelter on the Green. Victor, Donnie and Peter were there already, sitting on the bench.

'What's *she* doing here?' asked

74

Donnie rudely. 'She's not in our gang.'

Jinty snorted. 'I wouldn't be in your gang if you paid me, but you might be glad there's a Class Seven with you if Boney comes out.'

'You're a *girl*,' sneered Donnie. 'If you were in Class Five Million you'd *still* be a girl, and we don't need any girls holding our hands.'

'Give up fratching, you two,' growled Victor. '*I* don't mind having Jinty along—at least she's *seen* Boney, which is more than can be said for our gallant leader.'

'Talking of which, where *is* the genius?' asked Peter. 'It's freezing sitting here, waiting.'

'I bet he's not coming,' said Josh. 'He looked worried all day yesterday.'

Josh was wrong. Less than a minute later Ken Roe appeared, looking chipper. 'Morning, wolves,' he said, as a way of pleasing them.

'Morning, *sheep*,' mocked Victor. Miss Bowman had made the swot a member of her flock. 'You're looking quite fleecy this morning, if I may say so. Shall we go?'

75

Police Constable Lassiter wasn't on watch at the top of Shadows Lane, and there was no sign of the headmaster. Ken Roe screwed up his courage and marched his expedition into the tunnel of naked elms. The damp grey morning caused the lane to live up to its name.

'Feels like walking down a cow's throat,' quipped Victor.

'Been *down* one then, have you?' giggled Jinty.

'Once. I went right through and landed in a cowpat.'

'That's *disgusting*,' said the swot.

'Did someone just bleat?' asked the clown. They all laughed except Ken, who'd spotted the cottage.

'Is that *it*?' he murmured, trying to keep his voice steady.

'Yep,' chirped Victor. 'That's it, all right. You shove through the hedge, where the gate used to be.'

'What, *there*?' The swot pointed.

'Yes, *there*. Get on with it.'

Ken crept towards the leafy gap, parted some twigs with his hands and peered through. 'Looks deserted to me.'

'You wish,' growled Victor. 'Come

76

on, we're all waiting.'

The swot squeezed through the gap and stood, peering through the rhododendrons, trying not to shake. The others followed. 'You're our leader, Swot,' hissed Victor. 'What are your orders?'

'I . . . I'm not leading,' protested Ken. 'I said I'd be first in, that's all, and I was. What do *you* lot want to do?'

'Well, for a kick-off,' said Josh, 'I don't think we should go round the back. Jinty and I did that, and Boney nearly cut us off.'

'So what *do* we do?' asked Donny. 'No point just standing here, is there?'

Victor shook his head. ' 'Course not. What I thought we'd do is get as close to the house as we can without leaving the bushes, then start chucking things at the door. Pebbles and stuff. That should bring him out so we can get a good look without him spotting us. And if he comes down the steps, we scoot. What d'you reckon?'

'Sounds like a plan,' said Donny. The others nodded, and the group crept forward under the rhododendrons.

TWENTY-FIVE

KAPOWICE

The view from the window might be bleak, but Paul Bluet was having a good morning. The nightmares had left him alone for once, so that he'd slept. The stove was drawing well, starting to warm the kitchen. He'd cooked a pan of porridge, eaten half a bowlful and, so far, kept it down. It was a matter of pretending not to see the famished ghosts watching from dark corners, of distancing himself from their scandalized whispers by placing his thoughts elsewhere. It was unbelievably difficult, but he was getting better at it.

He was rinsing the bowl, imagining his body starting to fill out to a point where he'd begin to look like other people, when there was a loud bang. He jumped violently then froze, gripping the rim of the sink with both hands. In his mind he was beside his bunk at Kapowice, waiting helplessly to know whether this time

Bilciuk would choose his skull to blow to fragments with his Schmeisser. Butcher Bilciuk, whose habit it was on fine evenings to tour the barracks, select an inmate at random and murder him for the pleasure it gave him.

Now came a brief rattling, like hail blown onto a pane. It jerked him out of Kapowice, broke the paralysis. Bilciuk was no more here than the ghosts who watched him eat. The sound was repeated, punctuating his relief. The door, he told himself. Somebody's flinging gravel at the door. Those kids, I suppose. He needed more than anything to be left to heal, unseen and in his own time. The children didn't know that, of course: couldn't be expected to. Some words came into his head: they know not what they do, and that was exactly right, but they must be made to know, if he was ever to get well.

He shuffled along the stone-flagged passageway and cracked open the door.

TWENTY-SIX

SCARECROW HAIR

'Look!' shrilled the swot. 'It's opening.'

They paused, ready to flee, letting handfuls of dirt trickle to the ground as the door swung squeaking on stiff hinges.

'Oh, *crikey*,' moaned Peter. 'If that's a man, what the heck *happened* to him?'

The children stared aghast at the shape framed in the doorway. *Was* it a man? Could a man *be* that thin, like a skeleton somebody had hung clothes on? Or was it a scarecrow? It had scarecrow hair. Perhaps some prankster was behind, making it move.

As they stood, paralysed with horror, the apparition started down the steps, wading through the dirt and pebbles they'd thrown. It opened a toothless mouth and croaked, 'Go away, there's nothing here for you. Go and play.'

'Come on,' mumbled Victor, 'we

80

made a mistake. I don't know what's up with the poor chap, but he's real, not a ghost or a skeleton. Time to make ourselves scarce.'

They turned and ran, under the rhododendrons, through the gap in the hedge and back up Shadows Lane. They kept glancing behind, but Boney wasn't after them. In fact, they saw nobody at all till they reached the top, where Mrs Manders stood waiting with Constable Lassiter.

TWENTY-SEVEN

NOBODY FELT LIKE A WOLF

'What you lot been up to, eh?' demanded the constable. 'You've funny looks on your faces, I can tell you've done something you shouldn't.'

Victor shook his head. 'We only wanted to . . . there's a chap at the cottage, we seen him before, like a skeleton. We wanted to see him again, that's all.'

'So what did you do—knock?'

The boy stared at the ground. 'We chucked stuff.'

Mrs Manders let out a snort of disgust.

'At the door?' said the constable. 'You threw things at the door?'

Victor nodded. 'Yes, and then Boney came out.'

'*Boney?*' spluttered the grocer's wife.

'Yes. Only he's not a ghost like we thought, or a skeleton. He's a man. Looks ghastly, like he's got a terrible disease or something. We ran.'

Mrs Manders looked at Jinty. 'I *told* you, didn't I, in the shop? *Stay away from Shadows Lane*, I said. I bet you wish you'd taken notice now, don't you?'

Jinty nodded. 'I feel awful. He shouted *Go away* and he had no teeth. I wasn't scared any more, I was sorry.'

'You'd all better come with me,' growled Constable Lassiter, 'to the police station.'

'You're not *arresting* us?' croaked the swot. The others looked nervous too—nobody felt like a wolf.

The policeman shook his head. 'Not this time, but I need to talk to you: p'raps I should've done it sooner.' He looked at the grocer's wife. 'I'd appreciate it if you'd come along too, Mrs Manders.'

*   *   *

Extra chairs had to be carried into the living room so everybody could sit down. Mrs Lassiter went to put the kettle on.

'Now.' The constable looked at the semicircle of seated children. 'Who remembers that wartime poster that said *Walls Have Ears*?'

They all remembered.

'Well,' said Lassiter, 'we're not at war now, thank goodness, but walls *still* have ears, which means there's always somebody trying to learn other people's secrets so they can use them to cause a sensation.' He lowered his voice. 'We have a secret, here in Coney Cley. You kids discovered part of it by accident, down at Cornflower Cottage, so now I'm going to tell you the rest.

But you must never talk about it to anybody else, do you understand?'

They all nodded. Mrs Lassiter came with mugs of tea, which they sipped while the constable continued.

'The man you saw at Cornflower Cottage is called Paul Bluet. *Bluet* is French for "cornflower", and Paul's grandfather, who built the cottage, called it Cornflower Cottage for that reason. He lived on Jersey in the Channel Islands, and the cottage was his holiday home. After he died, nobody came to stay any more and the place became derelict.

'Now, as you probably know, the Channel Islands were occupied during the war by the Nazis, who made strict rules for the islanders to obey. One was, nobody could own a radio. Every radio had to be handed over to the Nazis, so that no islander could listen to the BBC news. But a few brave people hid radio sets in their houses. Paul Bluet was one of them. He'd listen to the news, then tell friends and neighbours what was happening in the world outside. The BBC told the truth, you see, and the Nazi radio did not.

'But somebody betrayed Paul Bluet: a neighbour, perhaps? The Nazis raided his house and found the radio. He was sent to a concentration camp in Poland, where he was starved and beaten and forced to do hard labour. He was a slave, like millions of others from all over Europe. Most died after a few months, but Paul survived. Just. When the Russian armies liberated the camp three years ago, they found a handful of survivors—skeletons in rags, who could barely stand. Paul Bluet was one of those.'

As the policeman paused to drink his tea, Josh heard a sniffling sound and saw that Victor was crying. He had his hands over his face, but he was crying all right. Jinty's cheeks were wet too. Josh had been fighting the aching lump in his own throat because big boys don't cry, but he broke down now.

Constable Lassiter gazed at his blubbing audience. He'd wanted to make them feel ashamed, but thought perhaps he'd overdone it. He looked at Mrs Manders, who nodded.

'I think they understand now, Mr Lassiter. Would you like me to finish off?'

He nodded back, pulling a large hanky out of his pocket. 'If you would, please, Mrs Manders. Here.' He passed the hanky to Victor. 'Dry your eyes, lad, and pass the hanky round.'

When everybody had resettled themselves, Mrs Manders spoke quietly. 'Paul Bluet, the man you know as Boney, survived, but the things he experienced in that camp left him very, very ill. Not just in his body, but in his mind as well. He can't face people, because of the way he looks. He can't go home to Jersey, because somebody there betrayed him—and he doesn't know who. He might pass that person every day on the street and not know. He couldn't bear the thought of that, so he came here—to his grandfather's cottage, where nobody knows him. He hoped to find peace, so that in time his body and mind might heal themselves.'

Jinty broke in. 'And we helped by pelting his door with stones.' She was crying again. 'We didn't *know*, honestly.

We thought he was . . .'

'I know, dear.' Mrs Manders nodded. 'We'd have liked to share the secret with the whole village, but then the story would have got out somehow, and Shadows Lane would've been crawling with reporters and sightseers and goodness knows who. Paul Bluet would never have known a moment's peace.'

'But *you* knew,' said Josh.

The woman nodded. 'We had to—we take Paul's rations to him every Saturday, after dark. Constable Lassiter knows, and the doctor, and the vicar.' She smiled. 'And now you. Can you keep the secret of Shadows Lane, d'you think? It's important.'

Josh nodded. 'Course we can, Mrs Manders, and we will. Is there some other way we can help, to make up for . . . you know?'

Constable Lassiter shook his head. 'Keep the secret, and stay away from Shadows Lane: that's the best way you can help.' He stood up. 'I think we're finished here. Run along now, the six of you, and remember—a brave man relies on your silence.'

TWENTY-EIGHT

FOR A SHEEP, I MEAN

'Come here, Swot.' Victor grabbed a fistful of Ken's collar and twisted it. They'd crossed the Stowmarket Road from the police house and entered the park. The clown slammed his victim's back against a tree. 'You're a peach and you know a secret,' he snarled, 'which means it won't be a secret for long.'

'I'm *not* a peach,' choked Ken. 'And *you're* not as tough as you pretend—I saw you blubbing.'

'That's *another* secret,' growled Victor, 'and if either of 'em gets out, us wolves'll know who to blame. Won't we, lads?'

Everybody nodded except Jinty, who muttered, 'I'm *not* a lad, but still.'

'You're not a wolf, either,' retorted the clown. 'I was talking to the wolves.' He released the swot, who fussed, straightening his tie. Victor glowered at him. 'One bleat out of you and it'll be your windpipe, not your tie.'

They made for the belvedere and sat in a half-circle on the bench. There wasn't much conversation. They were all seeing Boney inside their heads. Those fevered eyes in their deep sockets, that empty mouth.

'Must've been his, the tooth I found,' mumbled Josh. Jinty nodded.

'Shame we can't—you know—*do* something,' said Donnie after a while.

'There is *one* thing,' murmured Jinty.

Donnie looked at her. 'What?'

'We could write a letter of apology, post it to him.'

Peter looked doubtful. 'Postman'd know somebody was living there then,' he said. 'Envelope with *Paul Bluet, Cornflower Cottage, Shadows Lane, Coney Cley* on—it'd blow Boney's cover to bits, wouldn't it?'

Jinty blushed. 'Yes, *course* it would: what an ass I am.'

'We could still *write* one,' suggested Ken, 'only instead of posting it, we could take it to the shop and ask Mrs Manders to deliver it with Boney's rations. I'm sure she wouldn't mind.'

'Brilliant!' cried Victor. 'For a sheep, I mean. I vote we do it.' He looked at Jinty. 'You're a Class Seven, how about you doing the actual writing?'

Jinty shrugged. 'Yes, all right. And I'll let you all have a dekko at it before it goes to the shop.'

TWENTY-NINE

THE LETTER

Dear Mr Bluet,

My name is Jinty Linton. I'm eleven. This letter of apology is from me and my brother Josh, and from my brother's friends Victor Hammond, Peter Garfield, Donnie Walker and Ken Roe. We all go to Coney Cley JMI School, and we're the ones who threw dirt at your door to make you come out.

We didn't know who you were, or what happened to you in the war, but that's no excuse for what we did. It was thoughtless and stupid, and we wish we hadn't done it.

We asked Constable Lassiter if there was something we could do to make up for our silliness. He said we were to keep your secret, and stay away from Shadows Lane. I promise you we mean to do both those things. We wish you peace, and hope you'll soon be well.

Yours truly,
Jinty Linton

THIRTY

REALLY PRETTY

Victor nodded. 'Wizard letter, Jinty.' He handed it back to her. It was Monday morning, before the bell. They were in a corner of the covered area. The clown had read the letter out loud for the benefit of Peter and Donnie. Ken was somewhere else, he'd have to be given the gist later.

'I'll slip out at lunch time,' said Jinty, 'and give it to Mrs Manders.'

'No rush,' said Victor. 'It won't go till

Saturday, when they deliver Boney's rations.'

'What *I'm* hoping,' murmured Donnie, 'is that PC Lassiter hasn't told Old Nick what we got up to on Saturday.'

'Ooh, *don't*,' moaned Peter. 'Think about it—two on each hand to start the week.'

'We'll find out soon enough,' put in Josh, ' 'cause here's the bell.'

The pupils lined up and filed into assembly, class by class. The friends eyed the Head warily as he mounted the platform. He didn't look particularly upset, and in fact the gathering went off smoothly, with no mention of Shadows Lane.

'I had a very busy weekend,' said Miss Bowman, when she'd called the register. 'I've been sewing. See?' She lifted the lid of her high desk and took out two masks, which she held up. One was a sheep's face, the other a wolf's. They looked really good. 'I had twenty-one sheep to do, and four wolves,' she told them. 'Didn't get to bed till half-past one on Sunday morning, so I hope *you're* all going to work as hard to make our little play a success.'

Victor raised his hand. 'Can we try 'em on, miss?'

The teacher looked at him. 'They're not toys, Victor. We shan't be wearing them till the dress rehearsal, but I'm going to give them out now so we can check the fit. Hands up, the sheep.'

'Hooves, miss.'

'Did you speak, Victor?'

'Yes, miss, I said hooves. Sheep don't have hands.'

'No, and wolves don't speak.' Miss Bowman gazed at the clown. 'Do you remember what Kenneth said last Friday?'

'No, miss.'

'He said all angels are male. I've been thinking about that, and I may need to find a male to play our angel. I think you'd look *really* pretty in a bridesmaid's frock, Victor.'

Everybody laughed.

THIRTY-ONE

LIKE LARRY OLIVIER

The school always presented its Christmas Concert twice, on the last day of term. The afternoon performance was for staff and pupils, and for parents with small children who couldn't get out after tea. The evening performance was for everybody else, including any American airmen who might like to come, and the Mayor of Stowmarket if he wasn't too busy.

Backstage, the children whispered excitedly among themselves, while their teachers tried in vain to shush them. The afternoon show had gone down really well, especially Miss Bowman's novel take on the Nativity, so that the players were practically bursting to take the stage again.

Josh peeped through a gap in the curtain. The audience was pouring into St Hilda's as though Vera Lynn herself was topping the bill. He spotted the Mayor in the front pew, wearing his chain of office. There were a few Americans too, and a couple of those foreigners in black—the displaced persons—you saw patrolling the fence at the base.

When everybody was seated, the curtain went up on the school choir singing *While Shepherds Watched*. This was Miss Bowman's cue to get her class masked up and ready to go. Josh grinned behind his wolf's face. The masks looked absolutely wizard under the improvised lights. So did the white satin bridesmaid dress and paper wings Elaine Savage was wearing. *Wouldn't have looked the same on old Victor*, he thought.

It was another triumph. The actors moved like pros and delivered their lines like Larry Olivier. Nobody needed a prompt, and the choir sang its heart out. As the final notes of *O Come, All Ye Faithful* echoed among the roof-beams, the Mayor rose to his feet applauding. The entire audience followed his lead, clapping wildly. Jinty, a choir member, knew that if they weren't in church they'd have cheered and whistled too.

Taking his bow with the others, Josh turned to Victor and choked, 'I wish Boney'd been here.' The wolf mask hid his tears.

THIRTY-TWO

QUICK, BEFORE IT MELTS

So now it was the holidays, and Christmas. Shortages of almost everything made the festivity a travesty of its pre-war self, but only the adults knew this. To the children Christmas was magical, thanks to the thrift and ingenuity of their parents. Nogs and offcuts of wood became bright toys, festive dinners were contrived out of half-starved boiling fowls, and party tables groaned under the weight of mysterious sandwiches, gaudy eggless cakes and fruity-seeming trifles topped with gooey stuff pretending to be cream. It was all glossy top-show, but the kids didn't notice.

Then winter struck.

Nobody knew it at the time, but the winter of 1947 would go down in history as probably the severest of the century, with snow falling throughout January, February and March.

'Quick, before it melts!' cried Josh, the morning it started. He'd got a sledge for Christmas and was eager to try it out.

Coney Cley had no proper hill, just a gently sloping beet field beyond the church on Glebe Lane. Every child in the village was there that January morning, and a dad or two as well.

It wasn't very good. The gradient was shallow, the snow thick and feathery. You'd do a running push and pile on, only for the sledge to bog down after a few sluggish yards. It was about as exciting as painting the side of a barn, and a great deal colder. After an hour of wet socks and frozen fingers, Josh and Jinty decided to call it a day.

'I hope Mum didn't pay a lot for this sledge,' said Jinty as the pair trudged homeward, blowing into their hands. 'We haven't made much use of it.'

Josh shrugged. 'It might be better tomorrow, when people've trodden the snow down a bit.'

That night there was a hard frost, which probably improved the surface on the beet field, but by breakfast time it was snowing heavily, and any glazed runs would soon be obliterated.

Josh gazed through a window at the whirling flakes. 'Flipping school tomorrow,' he said gloomily.

'Brand-new term, love,' chirped his mother. 'You never know what wonderful things might happen.'

'Oh, yeah,' he said. 'I was forgetting that wonderful things keep happening at school, Mum. It's why kids go, isn't it?'

His mother shook her head. 'Sarcasm again, Joshua,' she reproved. 'Lowest form of wit, remember.'

'Hey!' Jinty grinned. 'If it snows all day, p'raps we won't be able to *get* to school.'

'This is England, sweetheart.' Her mother smiled, 'Not Siberia. *I* never had a single day off school because of snow.'

'No, but that was back in the olden days,' said Josh, 'before the Ice Age.' Mum swung a smack at his head, missing on purpose.

The pair helped her with the breakfast dishes, then went up to their rooms. Josh got out his Meccano set and started to build a crane. Jinty lay on her bed and stared at the ceiling.

I wonder how Boney's liking this weather? she mused.

THIRTY-THREE

MINCED PONY

'Hrrrmph! Good morning, boys and girls.'

'Good morning, Mr Nicholson. Good morning, friends.' A layer of snow covered the sloping windows in the roof, so that the light in the hall was poor.

'It's good to see all of you back safe

and sound after the holidays. In the course of those holidays, it was my pleasure to hear a number of very favourable comments about our Christmas concert. Many people thought it was the best they'd ever seen, and the Mayor of Stowmarket wrote to tell me how much he and the Lady Mayoress had enjoyed it. So jolly well done, everybody.'

'It was the masks,' whispered Josh to Victor. 'Especially our wolf ones.'

The clown nodded. 'I know. I was going to wear mine for sledging last Saturday, but my mum wouldn't let me: said it'd scare the little kids.' Miss Bowman had let her actors keep their masks as souvenirs. Josh had his hanging on the wall in his room.

Old Nick continued. 'Given the present weather, I'm sure you'll all be pleased to learn that the Council has agreed to convert our former air-raid shelter into an additional covered area for wet playtimes.' He smiled. 'Whether they'll actually get around to it before spring remains to be seen.' Some of the teachers tittered.

'What, no mention of Victor Hammond, the well-known planning consultant?' groused Victor to nobody in particular. 'P'raps they'll name it the Hammond Building though, eh?'

The Head's smile faded, but not because he'd overheard the clown. 'There's bad news too, I'm afraid. Fuel rationing, combined with difficult road conditions, has meant that supplies of coke for the school boiler are severely curtailed. From today, therefore, our heating will be turned off at one in the afternoon. Also from today, school meals will be meatless two days a week.'

'They're *all* meatless,' muttered Donny, 'unless a spoonful of minced pony counts as meat.'

'We will sing hymn number forty-six,' announced the Head. *'All Good Gifts Around Us.'*

THIRTY-FOUR

A PAIN IN THE NECK

With four inches of snow in the yard, morning break was indoors. There were battered board games, jigsaws with pieces missing, or pupils could choose among the few tatty books in the classroom library. It was just like a continuation of lesson time, except that the teacher was in the staffroom sipping tea, and they could talk among themselves.

'What a pain in the neck,' grumbled Peter. 'I'd have brought this week's *Hotspur* from home if I'd known.' The *Hotspur* was his favourite boys' paper.

'I don't know what's wrong with playing out in the snow,' said Josh.

Victor shook his head. 'It's the caretaker. Doesn't want a hundred and eighty pairs of wellies tracking puddles across his floors.'

'If he cleared the yard there wouldn't *be* any puddles,' growled Donny. 'Plus it'd give him something to do, now that he doesn't have to stoke the boiler in the afternoons.'

Ken didn't mind indoor breaks. As a swot in the yard, he'd have had handfuls of wet snow shoved down his neck, or been pelted with iceballs. He looked at Josh. 'Did we ever find out whether Boney got our letter of apology, Josh?'

Josh shook his head. 'Jinty gave it to Mrs Manders, who said she'd deliver it, but we've heard nothing since.'

'We should ask,' said Victor. 'I mean, we can't expect a reply or anything, but it'd be nice to know he got it.'

Josh nodded. 'I'll get Jinty to ask when we collect our rations on Saturday.'

The bell sounded for end of break. Monitors collected games and jigsaws and stacked them in a cupboard. Those who'd been reading marked their places with bits of paper and stowed the books in their desks. Miss Bowman burst in rubbing her hands: always an ominous sign.

'Sit up straight, everybody,' she

103

chirped. 'Open a window please, Elaine: it smells like a zoo in here. Now, clasp your hands on the desk in front of you, breathe deeply and put your thinking caps on. It's time for mental arithmetic.'

'Time for mental *treatment*, if you ask me,' muttered the clown as an icy draught caressed his neck.

THIRTY-FIVE

TRAPPED

Paul Bluet shuffled his chair closer to the stove.

Cornflower Cottage was a holiday home, it wasn't designed to be occupied in winter. Doors and windows hung loose in their frames, so that the east wind rattled them and blew draughts through the rooms. The man rewrapped the blanket round his wasted shoulders before smoothing out the crumpled paper he was holding. He tilted it to catch the grey light from the window and read, his lips moving to form words he'd read at least forty times.

Dear Mr Bluet,
My name is Jinty Linton. I'm eleven. This letter of apology . . .

There were tears on his cheeks when he reached the signature. He cried for Jinty and her friends because they knew nothing, and for all those children at Kapowice who'd known more than any child should know before they died.

He folded the letter and sat for a while, staring at the fire. If he gazed long enough, he'd start seeing their faces. Old men's faces on the shoulders of children, shuffling away to become part of the Final Solution.

He shook his head. It does no good, *he told himself.* They're gone, nothing will bring them back. What you must do is live, because as long as you're alive, they won't be forgotten.

He rose on skeletal legs, slipped the letter under the clock and tottered across to the window, clutching the blanket to his throat with one hand. Three o'clock and still snowing. The grocer had struggled to carry his supplies down Shadows Lane last Saturday, and it had snowed for two days since then. He knew he ought to leave the cottage while he could, take a room at the Fox and Grapes till a thaw set in, but he couldn't. He couldn't.

Well, *look* at me. Could you face people with a face like mine: a body like mine? Could you cope with their curiosity, their questions, asked and unasked? Could you? Of course you couldn't, it's impossible. I'm trapped, you see. In this body, in this cottage. They let me out of Kapowice, but they forgot to let Kapowice out of me.

THIRTY-SIX

COLOURFUL LANGUAGE

Old Nick was absent on Tuesday morning. Doggy Barker was Deputy Head, so he took assembly. 'The Stowmarket Road is blocked by snow,' he announced, 'and the Council has no petrol for its snowplough.' Muted mirth from some of the teachers. 'A delivery of fuel *was* expected but it didn't arrive, because the Stowmarket Road is blocked by snow.'

The sounds of mirth became less muted. Doggy flushed, coughed and continued. 'Mr Nicholson is unable to be with us . . .'

'*Because the Stowmarket Road is blocked by snow,*' intoned the teachers in unison. The children looked astonished for a moment, then gasped and laughed. They knew the teachers wouldn't have dared do such a thing if Old Nick had been here.

Doggy strode to the edge of the platform, where he stood frowning over everybody's heads till the noise faded away. '. . . but he telephoned to me a while ago to say he feels sure everybody at Coney Cley JMI School will pull together to keep things ticking over through these difficult times. Let us sing hymn number fifty-three: *From Greenland's Icy Mountains.*'

Doggy strode into the classroom looking furious, and for once his pupils knew he wasn't angry with *them*. He was angry with Mr Ball the PT teacher who had sung, quite distinctly, *England's Icy Mountains* instead of *Greenland's*.

Jinty nudged her best friend. 'I never knew teachers got mad with each *other*,' she whispered.

'I didn't know they could be *naughty*,' giggled Sandra. 'D'you think he'll give old Cannon a detention?' Cannon was Mr Ball's nickname.

'A hundred lines, I should think,' hissed Jinty. *'I must not change the words of hymns, it sets a bad example.'*

It was English. Doggy looked out of the window at the relentlessly falling flakes. 'I want each of you to produce me an essay entitled *A Snowy Day*,' he said. 'Try to use colourful language: *a skyful of feathers. The park, iced like a wedding cake. Bird footprints are arrows that point the way it went.'*

'*The village pond*,' murmured Sandra,

'like a wellyful of tapioca.'

Doggy glanced up sharply. 'Did you speak, Sandra Tasker?'

'No, sir.'

THIRTY-SEVEN

YANKS, GO HOME

Mr Slingsby, the caretaker, spent the first half of the morning clearing snow off the yard with a shovel. He wasn't happy at his work, but Doggy wanted the children to have an outdoor playtime so they could let off steam. By half-past ten, the yard was a square of gleaming tarmac with a border of piled-up snow. *I just hope it doesn't start snowing again*, the caretaker thought, surveying his work.

Jinty and Sandra loitered in the gateway. A massive snowball fight was in progress, and this was the best spot to avoid it. There was no traffic on Glebe Lane, but now and then a villager would trudge by in gumboots, heading for Manders' shop on the High Street.

Presently the two girls heard a motor in the distance. Something was approaching along Glebe Lane. 'Sounds like a big lorry,' said Jinty.

Sandra nodded. 'Slow, whatever it is.'

When the vehicle came into view, they saw that it was a great yellow snowplough. As it drew near, the roar of its engine brought children running to the gate. 'It's not the Council,' said a boy. 'It's the Americans, *look*.'

It was. Two airmen in flying jackets sat in the high cab. Behind the plough marched a squad of men in black, with shovels on their shoulders like rifles. 'DPs,' said Donnie.

Josh looked puzzled. 'They're not ploughing, are they? Look, the blade's raised.'

'I think I know why,' said Sandra. 'They're not bothering with Glebe Lane, they're going to do the High Street because it's the Stowmarket Road. I bet the Council asked them to.'

As the children watched, the

machine hung a ponderous right in front of the Green and followed the curve, past the Fox and Grapes and right again onto the High Street. A group led by Victor left the yard and ran to the corner. This was forbidden, but they were rewarded by seeing the blade descend. Sandra's guess had been right.

Ken Roe shook his head. 'I wonder if whoever daubed *YANKS, GO HOME* on the side of the village hall is glad they stayed?' he said.

THIRTY-EIGHT

MYRON PIENKOWSKI

The driver braked, leaned out of his cab and shouted over the engine noise. 'C'mon, guys: try to keep up. You gotta chip out all of that hard-packed ice and chuck it on the side.'

The DPs didn't understand a word he said, but it was plain from his gestures what he expected of them.

The plough cut through the deep snow and flung it to left and right, but it left a thin layer of ice on the tarmac which only shovels could dislodge. It was impossible to keep up with the plough of course, but their jobs with the US military were all these men now had, so they were going to raise a sweat trying.

Myron Pienkowski jabbed his blade at a stubborn lump, cursing the driver under his breath. He hated Americans and Russians equally.

'*Swine*,' he spat. 'Sitting up there in your cab like a Maharajah on an elephant, issuing orders. You're only a private, and a *Jewish* one at that. You wouldn't have been so high and mighty under the Reich, by Jiminy you wouldn't. *You'd* have been the one with the shovel there, my smug friend.' He straightened his aching back and looked down the road. It was a long, long way to Stowmarket.

*   *   *

Back in the schoolyard, playtime was over. Josh's class filed back to the classroom, where Miss Bowman was waiting to pounce.

'I see your flock still follows you into danger, Victor Hammond.'

'I don't know what you mean, miss.'

'You left the yard, I was watching from the staffroom window. Others followed as usual.'

'Yes, but it was the snowplough, miss. The Americans. We wanted to see where they'd go.'

'Where the Americans went was none of your business, Victor. Your business is to obey school rules, which are there for your safety.'

'Yes, miss, sorry. Miss?'

'What is it?'

'What does DP mean, miss?'

'Displaced Person.'

'Yes, but what does it *mean*? How do people *get* displaced, miss? Where do they come from, and why are they here?'

The teacher shook her head. 'It was the war, Victor. In wartime, countless thousands of people are forced to abandon their homes, for all sorts of reasons. They may be afraid of being bombed, or shot, or forced into slavery. So they take to the roads, carrying their babies and their possessions in carts or on their backs. Others are rounded up for being Jews or gypsies or communists and herded into concentration camps. And when the war's over, they find they can't go home. Their house is no longer standing, or a new government doesn't want them back, or things have changed in their country and they don't want to live there any more. They've become displaced. No home, no job, no family. So we give them camps to live in, and food to eat, and if we can we find work for them. The DPs we see in Coney Cley are mostly Polish or Ukrainian. They work for the Americans, out at the airbase.'

'Oh.' Victor nodded. 'So they're unlucky then, same as Boney?' He heard Josh gasp, and realized what he'd done.

Miss Bowman frowned. '*Who?*'

'Er . . . Boney, miss. Napoleon Bonaparte. *He* couldn't go home either, 'cause they put him on an island.'

'Hmmm. Not *quite* the same, Victor: Napoleon *deserved* his exile, didn't he? The DPs don't.'

THIRTY-NINE

OOMIFLOOMI

'I hate cheese pie,' moaned Donnie, poking at it with his fork. 'So does every kid in the school, so why do they keep dishing it up?'

' 'Cause there are meatless days, you dope,' growled Victor, who was feeling smug at the brilliant way he'd covered his Boney slip. 'What would *you* put in—fat juicy slugs?'

'Ugh, *shut* up.' Donnie pushed his plate away.

'My mum reckons we'll be eating whale soon.' Peter grinned. 'She heard it on the news.' Peter's mother was the school cook.

'*Whale?*' gasped a boy next to him. 'I'd rather have the cheese pie—can't stand fish.'

Ken Roe sighed and put down his fork. 'A whale isn't a *fish*, you peasant,' he sneered, 'it's a mammal. Everybody knows that.'

'Still wouldn't want to eat it,' said the boy.

The swot shrugged. 'The Inuit thrive on it.'

Victor looked at him. 'The *what*?'

'The Inuit. *You* probably call them Eskimos.'

'If you don't quit showing off,' said the clown, 'you'll get a mouthful of my oomifloomi—you probably call it my fist.'

Lunch over, the pupils were released into the yard. It was snowing again. A thin covering hid the tarmac. Victor scraped a lump together with the side of his welly, scooped it up and moulded it into a firm ball. 'Now, where's that ruddy Inuit?'

Ken was by the gate, looking up with his mouth open, eating snowflakes. Victor's icy missile smacked into his ear. He howled and bent forward, one hand clamped over the injured part.

Victor grinned and yelled, 'Gotcha, you mammal,' just as Mr Nicholson strode into the yard.

When he came out of the Head's study ten minutes later, the clown's happy mood had evaporated, and he couldn't open his hands to wipe his eyes. Old Nick's magic wand had made oomifloomis of them both.

FORTY

ONE MORE BRAIN CELL

Before the school day ended, the American snowplough had met the Council machine coming the other way, and the Stowmarket Road was open. Old Nick, who had had to walk most of the way to school, was able to catch a bus home.

'I hope it gets stuck halfway,' muttered Victor, 'and they find his body next spring, and it turns out he's eaten the other passengers.' He still couldn't uncurl his hands.

'Well, why not?' grinned Josh. 'Passengers are mammals, aren't they, same as whales. If you can eat one, why not the other?'

Jinty scowled at her brother. 'You've got a morbid imagination, Josh,' she told him. 'Dead Cat Vicarage—I haven't forgotten *that*! Now cannibal headmasters. If you're not careful, men in white coats'll come and take you away.' She looked at Victor. 'I thought we might drop in on Mrs Manders now the road's clear, ask about our letter.'

Victor nodded. 'Wizard idea, Jinty. I sometimes think that if you had one more brain cell, you'd be a boy.'

'Yes, and if *you* had it instead it'd be your first,' growled Jinty.

A large van was parked outside Manders'. It hadn't been able to reach the kerb, because of the snowbank the plough had left. Its rear doors stood open, and the driver and Mr Manders were going back and forth through a gap they'd dug in the snowbank, carrying stuff into the shop.

'Afternoon, Mr Manders,' called Jinty as the trio approached. 'You look busy.'

'We *are* busy,' said the grocer. 'What do you kids want?'

'Just a word with Mrs Manders,' Jinty replied, 'if that's all right.'

Manders paused, hugging a net of onions to his chest. 'As a matter of fact, it isn't,' he panted. 'Not just now. This delivery has come in the nick of time, and my wife is busy re-stocking our shelves. What's this word *about*—perhaps *I* can help.'

'It's just . . .' Jinty waited till the driver disappeared inside the shop. 'We wanted to ask if Mrs Manders gave Bo . . . gave Mr Bluet our letter of apology.'

'*I* gave it to him,' said Manders. 'I doubt there'll be a reply, if that's what you're waiting for.'

'No, no.' Jinty shook her head. 'We weren't expecting one.' The driver reappeared. 'We'll be off then, Mr Manders—our mums'll be wondering where we've got to. Cheerio—I'm glad you got your delivery.'

They retraced their steps to Glebe Lane, walking in the road to avoid the uncleared pavement. 'So he got it,' said Victor. 'I'm glad. Not that it makes up for what we did.'

Josh pulled a face. 'It *doesn't*, does it? I can't stop thinking about him. I wish we could *do* something, apart from keeping his secret.'

'Which *I* nearly blabbed to Miss Bowman,' said the clown ruefully. 'On the other hand, I suppose you could say that I've suffered for it since.'

'On *both* hands, actually,' said Josh, smiling.

FORTY-ONE

A YARDFUL OF LAUGHING HYENAS

Deep snow's fun for about a week. Children revel in it. Adults grumble and claim to hate it, but deep down they're enjoying it because it brings something a bit different into their boring lives. Trains and buses run late or don't turn up at all, so there's an excuse for not getting to work on time, or even for having a day off. There are garden paths to be kept clear, and a wife can feel heroic just struggling home with a basket of groceries.

More than a week, and the fun tends to fade away.

It snowed every day that week, and the week after, and it froze hard every night. And this wasn't just Coney Cley, it was all over the country. Food and fuel, already rationed, began to run low. So did salt to treat road surfaces. Isolated communities were cut off, and the BBC news ran stories about the RAF dropping food from aeroplanes.

'Never mind.' Jill Linton smiled, as the big freeze entered its third week. It was breakfast time, Monday. 'This sort of weather never lasts more than a week or two in England. You'll see— the thaw's bound to set in tomorrow or the day after.'

'That's what you said *last* Monday, Mum,' muttered Josh, 'and look at it.' Feathery flakes fell thickly beyond a grey kitchen window on which the frost-patterns were still melting.

Jinty bit into her toast. 'I passed old Doggy chatting to Cannon in the corridor on Friday,' she mumbled, talking with her mouth full. 'He said something about the school having to close if it stays cold and the coke lorry can't get through.'

Josh pulled a face. 'Let's hope it closes today, so we don't have to turn up in Dad's old trousers.' Their mother had spent part of the weekend cutting down and sewing two pairs of her late husband's flannels, to cover those parts of the children's legs left exposed by uniform skirts and short trousers. They'd tried them on in front of the dressing-table mirror.

'We look like a pair of those circus clowns whose baggy pants explode in the ring,' complained Josh. 'I can't go to school looking like this—the kids'd laugh themselves silly.'

'The kids'll have chapped knees and sore rings round their legs where the tops of their wellies chafe,' retorted his mother. 'You won't.' Now she shook her head. 'If school was closed today, Joshua, Mr Nicholson would have made sure everybody knew. And you'll be glad of the long trousers when you get there warm and dry.'

So sister and brother pulled the trousers on over their ordinary clothes, each giggling at the other's appearance. 'I'm Charlie Chaplin,' said Jinty, 'and you can be The Kid. We'll practise the walk on the way.'

The snow was too deep to practise any walk except giant footsteps, but it turned out that their mother was right—they were both staying dry and warm in the baggy old pants.

'Sis?' said Josh, as they turned onto Glebe Lane.

'What?'

'Do you *like* having a secret from Mum and everybody?'

Jinty shrugged. 'I did at first. It felt as if I was cleverer than them in some way, and . . . special. You know: *A brave man relies on your silence.* So yes, I felt special.' She pulled a face. 'I'm not sure now, though. What I think now is, it's no good knowing a secret if nobody *knows* you know it. I keep wanting to say, *I know something you don't know,* especially to Mum, but once you've said that, they're bound to get the rest of it out of you pretty quickly. So no, Josh—I *don't* like our secret, but we're stuck with it, aren't we? I mean, I don't think for a minute Mum'd blab if we explained, but a promise is a promise.'

'Yes, and a yardful of laughing hyenas is a yardful of laughing hyenas,' warned Josh as the school gate loomed. They took deep breaths and strode out to face their audience.

FORTY-TWO

THE LINTON LOOK

'All stop work,' said Jinty's teacher. 'Put your pens down.' It was half-past two. The heating had gone off at one o'clock, and now it was freezing in school. Doggy's breath hung in a cloud around his head. 'Stand up.'

Class Seven stood, shivering. Jinty leaned towards Sandra. 'I bet he's sending us home,' she whispered.

'Wouldn't that be super?' Sandra replied.

'Jumping on the spot, clapping your hands above your heads like this, *begin*.' Doggy started jumping and clapping. The children joined in, shaking up the baked fish roll they'd eaten for dinner.

'Pity,' panted Sandra, when they'd bounced for a full minute.

'Yes, isn't it?' gasped Jinty.

'And *stop*,' said Doggy. Everybody stopped. The teacher grinned. 'Warmer now, are we?'

'Yes, sir,' murmured some of the class.

'Good. Now do this with your arms.' He flung his arms wide, then swung them in an arc across his body to slap himself under the armpits, before extending them and repeating the exercise. Everybody copied him.

'And *stop*,' said Doggy after twenty slaps. 'All right. Sit down and carry on.' Everybody felt warmer, but only a bit.

They were copying a poem from the blackboard: *Roundabouts and Swings*. Jinty dipped her pen and wrote the

125

line: *And it's bread and bacon mostly*. The chap in the poem was moaning because he lived on bacon a lot of the time. *You're lucky*, she thought. *You should try making two ounces last a week*. Maybe she'd write a poem of her own: *And it's prunes and mousetrap mostly* . . . Yes, maybe she would.

Playtime arrived. Jinty could have done without it. The weather was rotten as usual, and she and Josh were bound to be jeered again for their exploding trousers.

'Don't put 'em on,' suggested Sandra. 'Leave 'em in the cloakroom.'

Jinty shook her head. 'I *can't*. Josh'll have his on, and I'm not leaving him to be laughed at by himself.'

To her surprise and relief, nobody laughed. 'Novelty's worn off,' said Sandra. 'By tomorrow they'll have forgotten you ever dressed any other way.'

Crossing the yard at home time, Josh and Jinty were accosted by Peter Garfield. 'Uh . . . my mum wants a word with you,' he mumbled, 'in the kitchen.'

126

Jinty's heart lurched. 'It's not about . . .?'

'Boney? No, don't worry, it's something else.'

'Phew!'

They followed him round the back of the school. Mrs Garfield was in the kitchen doorway. She smiled. 'What a clever idea those trousers are. I expect your mum made them for you, eh?'

Jinty nodded. 'They were Dad's. Mum shortened them and took them in.'

The cook nodded. 'Clever lady, your mum. D'you think . . . if I brought her a pair of Mr Garfield's, would she alter them to fit Peter? I'd pay her, of course.'

Jinty nodded. 'Don't see why not, Mrs Garfield.'

'Will you mention it to her, love, when you get home?'

'Course.'

'Whoever would've thought it?' chuckled Jinty, walking home. 'We begin the day as the school joke, and end by starting a brand-new fashion.' She indicated Josh with a sweep of her hand. 'Ladies and Gentlemen—the Linton Look.'

FORTY-THREE

STRINGER

Sometimes it looked as if the cold snap was breaking down. There'd come a morning when the snow stopped, the sky cleared and a watery sun set icicles dripping on everybody's eaves. Passing a neighbour on the road, somebody would say, 'It's here at last then, the thaw.'

It wasn't. That night it would freeze again, and in the morning the dirty old snow was covered by a fresh white blanket, the icicles longer than ever. Even the children were getting sick of it.

School didn't close, though there were empty seats in every classroom as pupils went down with bronchitis, whooping cough and croup. The Council struggled to keep the

Stowmarket Road open, and deliveries of food and fuel got through from time to time. There was no more help from the Americans, whose plough was needed all day every day to keep the runways clear.

The Linton Look caught on. Nobody called it that, but a dozen mothers followed in Mrs Garfield's footsteps, arriving at the Lintons' door with pairs of old trousers to be altered. Soon, pupils who'd jeered at Josh and Jinty appeared in the schoolyard wearing baggy old pants of their own.

On the last Saturday in January, Josh and Jinty trudged along to Manders' shop pulling the sledge, which slid freely over tracks of beaten snow where people had walked.

It was early, and there were no other customers. While Josh gave their mother's order to the grocer, Jinty spoke to Mrs Manders, who was filling a box. 'Is that for Mr Bluet?' she asked.

Mrs Manders straightened up, sighing. 'Yes, love, but goodness knows how we're going to get it down Shadows Lane. My husband only just managed last week, and it's snowed heavens high since then.'

'Does he use the van?'

'No. Can you imagine trying to drive a little van through this stuff, especially at night. He'd get stuck and die of frostbite.'

'So he walks, carrying that box?'

'Ssssh!' warned Mrs Manders. A customer was on the doormat, stamping his feet.

Jinty pretended to look at some tins on a shelf. When the man had gone she said, 'Wouldn't it be safer if Mr Bluet stayed somewhere else, just till the snow melts?'

Mrs Manders nodded. 'Of course it would. My husband mentioned it, but Paul's mixed up in his head. Can't face people. Won't budge. No.' She shook her head. 'We'll just have to manage, and hope the thaw comes soon.'

Outside, Jinty told Josh what Mrs Manders had said. 'I bet you and I could get Boney's rations down the lane easier than old Manders,' she said.

Josh nodded. 'We probably could, Sis, if it hadn't to be done after dark.

We'd have to tell Mum what we were doing, so the secret would be out, and even then she might not let us go.'

'I know.'

They were opposite the Fox and Grapes when a man approached them. 'Excuse me?'

The pair looked at him. A tall, thin man with a long nose and reddish hair. He didn't live in the village.

'What d'you want?' asked Jinty.

The man grinned. 'A few words, that's all.' He nodded at the sledge. 'Clever way to carry the shopping. Sort of thing I'm looking for.'

'You're looking for a sledge?' asked Josh.

The man chuckled. 'No, son, I don't mean that. Let me explain.' He produced a wallet and slid out a small card. 'My name's Brian Palgrave, see?' He showed them the card. 'I'm a reporter—what they call a stringer. It's my job to sniff out interesting stories for the big London paper I work for.' He smiled. '*Interesting* at the moment means anything to do with the big freeze—like your Eskimo way of

131

hauling the rations. A snapshot of the two of you with that sledge could make the front page on a slow day.'

Jinty frowned. 'You haven't got a camera.'

Palgrave shook his head. 'No, I don't mean I'm going to take your picture this minute, sweetheart. What I mean is, our readers love anything unusual about the freeze. How it's affecting people in different parts of the country: disrupting their routines, forcing them to improvise.' He shrugged. 'You look like bright kids. I hoped you might put me in the way of something interesting about Coney Cley.' He grinned. 'I've been known to pay half a crown for a good lead.'

'Half a *crown*?' gasped Josh. 'Just for—*Ow!*'

Jinty jabbed him in the ribs. 'We don't know anything,' she told the reporter. 'Nothing ever happens here.' She grabbed a fistful of her brother's sleeve. 'Come *on*, Josh.'

FORTY-FOUR

TWO HALF-CROWNS FOR A START

'What the heck did you think you were *doing*?' demanded Jinty, when they'd turned onto Hayfield Lane.

Josh scowled. 'What d'you mean? I only wanted to know about the half-crowns. It was *rude*, the way you talked to him. *And* dragging me away like that. I've a good mind to go back.'

Jinty grabbed his sleeve again. 'You'll do nothing of the sort, Josh,' she hissed. 'Have you forgotten we're supposed to be guarding a secret? Did the thought of half a crown drive it clean out of your head?'

Josh jerked free of her grip. 'I wouldn't have told him about *Boney*, you fathead. What d'you think I am? I could've told about school, how we have to do PT in the classroom so we don't freeze. Or Mum and the Linton Look. There's *two* half-crowns for a start.'

Jinty shook her head. 'He'd not pay good money for stuff like that. He's *fishing*, Josh. Sticking his long nose into people's business, looking for something he can whip up into a sensation. We mustn't encourage him. *You* might not peach on Boney for half a crown, but somebody else might.'

'*Who?*' cried Josh. 'Manders? PC Lassiter? The *vicar?*'

Jinty shook her head again. 'Stories leak out, Josh. Better for everybody if Stringer Palgrave finds Coney Cley dead boring and goes away. Come on.' She trudged on with the sledge. Josh trailed behind.

*   *   *

In the bar of the Fox and Grapes, Brian Palgrave sat at a corner table thinking about Jinty, though he didn't know her name. *We don't know anything*, she'd said. *Nothing ever happens here*. He smiled to himself. 'Stuff happens everywhere, sweetheart,' he murmured into his beer. 'And whatever happens, Brian Palgrave's the man to sniff it out. By golly he is.'

FORTY-FIVE

DAYLIGHT ROBBERY

Saul Manders pulled out his watch and looked at it. Ten to four. The shop was open till four on Saturdays, but there'd been no customer in the past hour, it was dark outside and it'd just started snowing again. 'Nobody's going to come now, love,' he told his wife. 'I'm closing so I can get off with Paul's order.'

Mrs Manders nodded. 'Yes, you get off. I'll lock up.' She gave him an anxious look. 'You *will* be careful, won't you?'

He nodded, lifting the box. 'Phone Lassiter if I'm not back by five-thirty.'

He walked out into the snow. Mrs Manders was closing the door when a tall figure loomed in the gaslight. A stranger with a long nose. 'Sorry to come at the last minute, sweetheart, but do you happen to have twenty Senior Service?'

'*Twenty?*' She didn't like strangers calling her sweetheart. 'I don't have twenty for a regular customer, which you're not. I can let you have five.'

The man shrugged. 'Five it is, then. And a tube of lighter fuel.' He smiled. 'Do you mean to bring them out to me, or may I come inside?'

Mrs Manders stepped aside. 'I suppose you'd better come in a minute.'

'Thanks.' He stood on the mat, mopping his red hair with a hanky while she hunted for lighter fuel. 'Must be grim for you lately,' he said, 'what with shortages, late deliveries, only shop in the village.' He shook his head. 'I bet there are stories you could tell, eh?'

'Maybe,' she said, 'if I was the storytelling sort. Here y'are.' She handed him a paper bag. 'Five Seniors, lighter fuel, that'll be tenpence ha'penny.'

'*Tenpence ha'penny* for five fags?'

'And fuel.'

'It'd be daylight robbery if it wasn't dark,' the man growled. 'At least Dick Turpin had the grace to wear a mask.'

Mrs Manders looked at him. 'You said it yourself—only shop in the village. And now it's shut.'

'All right, all right—I'm going.' He turned in the doorway. 'By the way, did I see somebody leave as I was crossing the road—chap with a big box?'

'I don't know,' said Mrs Manders, brandishing the key. '*Did* you?'

FORTY-SIX

LURKING UNDER ELMS

Saul Manders made his way past the Green and turned left along the Stowmarket Road. It wasn't so bad underfoot: the boots of passers-by had left a narrow track of compacted snow, and so far the fresh fall had laid only half an inch of fluffy stuff on top.

It was when he crossed the road and

entered Shadows Lane that things became difficult. Nobody had walked here since his own journey a week ago. The footprints he'd left then were buried under at least a foot of undisturbed snow, and this was deepening every minute.

The box, which had felt reasonably light to start with, was making his arms ache. He set it down to rest them, and it sank four inches into the snow. He stood for a minute, massaging the small of his back and gazing down the lane, before continuing.

He was about halfway down, breathing hard but coping, when he ran into a real obstacle. There was a break in the double row of elms at this point, and a cross-wind had blown snow through it to build a five-foot drift right across the lane: a drift that was all but invisible in the dark. He backed off with an oath. A clot of snow had found the gap between the top of his boot and his sock and was sending an icy trickle over his ankle.

Damn. He crabbed to his left and tried again. *Just as deep—what about this side?* He crabbed right. *Same. All right, then—have to wade through.*

He moved into the drift, hoping it would bear his weight so he could scramble over. It wouldn't. His first couple of steps took him waist-deep. His next two, which were almost impossible to take because of the weight of snow his legs were pushing, left him up to his armpits, holding the box clear, unable to progress another inch. The insides of his boots were packed with a freezing mush. Cold soaked through his woollen topcoat, making him gasp. The only way he could move was backwards, the way he'd come. Having no choice, he retreated. Clear of the drift he stood shivering, staring down the lane, numb with cold and defeat. Lumps of snow clung to his coat and trousers. He bent and started to knock them off, mechanically, his mind on the man whose supplies he'd abandoned on top of the drift.

What's he got left at the cottage? Can't be much. Is there another way to reach him? Maybe somebody else would make a better job of getting through than I have. A younger man. I must get back, tell Lassiter, he'll think of something. Oh God, how much longer can this wretched weather last?

As though to mock him, the wind suddenly strengthened. It drove flying snow into the grocer's face as he slogged back up Shadows Lane. Head down, he didn't notice the man lurking under elms near the junction. As Manders turned onto the Stowmarket Road, the lurker set off down Shadows Lane, following his long nose and the instinct for which he was famous. There was a story here, and Brian Palgrave was determined to track it down.

FORTY-SEVEN

TOODLE PIP

Josh stuck his head round Jinty's door. 'Have you seen the weather?'

His sister looked up from the jigsaw

she was doing. 'Yes, I have, and it's its usual beastly self: why?'

'I'm thinking about Mr Manders, Sis. He's got Boney's stuff to deliver. Just think what Shadows Lane'll be like now. What if he gets stuck or falls down or something? He's pretty old. He could die, like that man on the news.'

Jinty got up and crossed to her window. The wind was blowing snow in clouds across the garden. 'I suppose he could, Josh, but Mrs Manders knows that. She'll raise the alarm if he's not back by a certain time.'

Josh shook his head. 'You told me she didn't know how they'd get the stuff down Shadows Lane. I wonder if she was hoping we'd offer to help.'

Jinty shook her head. 'I don't think so, Josh. She knows Mum wouldn't let us, especially since she doesn't even *know* about Boney.'

'Well, I still think we should've offered.' He dropped his voice. 'Mum's popped next door to see Mrs Lewis. Said she'd just be a minute, but she'll be half an hour at least because old

Lewis always puts the kettle on, so I think I'll scoot along to Shadows Lane, make sure everything's all right. I can do it in well under half an hour.'

Jinty shook her head. 'No, you *can't*, Josh, not in deep snow. And anyway, what if Mum's *not* half an hour? What am I supposed to tell her, without mentioning Boney?'

Josh grinned. 'If you stay up here, she'll think I'm still in my room. And anyway, I'll be back before her, you'll see. Toodle pip.' She heard him go downstairs.

I should run next door, she told herself. *Get Mum. She'll stop him, but then she'll want to know where he was going, and why, and then the secret'll be out.*

As she stood, torn between a duty of care and a promise, she heard the front door close. Running into her mother's room, she looked out in time to see her brother butting into the blizzard with his head down.

FORTY-EIGHT

A GALLANT FAILURE

Brian Palgrave trudged down Shadows Lane with the wind behind him, writing Monday's story in his head.

Shadows Lane is well named, for it boasts no streetlamps. Few if any of Coney Cley's inhabitants pass this way in wintertime, especially after dark, and more especially when the lane is clogged with snow. There is a single gallant exception: the village grocer, whom I saw carrying a box of provisions on foot, after dark and through a raging blizzard, so that his customer should not go hungry.

He smiled to himself. *Good first para, Brian old son. The editor will bite your hand off for this one.* He knew absolutely nothing about the village grocer *or* his customer: he'd learned the name of the lane only a minute ago by kicking caked ice off the sign at the top. He'd no idea how long Shadows Lane was, or how many people lived here, but a good journalist needs very few facts to build a story on. Often, the best parts are the ones he makes up.

Can't be far, he thought. *The old geezer wasn't down here five minutes. His prints won't have filled in. I'll track him and talk to the customer.*

When Palgrave reached the drift, he noticed the tell-tale marks of Manders' failure: the man-size indentation further along the drift, the tumbled clots and there, on top of the drift, the box. He swore, knowing that even if he got through, he'd have little chance of finding the customer. There'd be no footprints to follow, and he had no way of knowing there was only the one cottage.

He backed off, adjusting the piece he'd write. *A Gallant Failure*, that'd be the heading. He'd mention Captain Scott, Captain Oates. Like the grocer, they'd failed in their objective, but they were heroes all the same.

He'd turned to start back when the wind gusted, there was a fearful rending noise, and a torn-off elm branch struck him across the shoulders and drove him unconscious into the snow.

FORTY-NINE

HAVING KITTENS

At the top of Shadows Lane, Josh thought: *If old Manders is still down there, there'll be just the one set of footprints: his, going down. I'll walk in them, like King Wenceslas's page in the carol, see if I can help. If he's been to Boney's and come back I'll see two sets, and I'll know I can stop worrying and go home.*

This sounded foolproof, but wasn't. The light was bad, and the blizzard was filling in the prints, but it seemed to Josh there were two sets going down. *Maybe Mrs Manders came with her husband*, he mused. But that wouldn't work, because only one person had returned. *Have to take a butcher's*, he decided, and set off down the lane.

Like the grocer and the journalist

before him, he didn't see the drift till he ploughed into it. *Aw, heck!* He stepped back, clawing snow out of the top of his welly. As he straightened up, he saw a thick tree branch embedded in the drift. The whirling flakes made him half blind, but there seemed to be part of a sleeve as well, with a hand poking out.

'Mr Manders!' He waded in, scooping snow from around the sleeve. 'Are you all right?' *What a stupid question*, he thought, and yelled 'Can you hear me?' instead. Digging frantically with freezing hands, he uncovered the rest of the arm, a shoulder, and finally a face.

Brushing snow from the eyes and nose, Josh recognized the journalist who'd offered half-crowns. He couldn't tell if the man was breathing, but the open mouth was crammed with snow. He hooked it out with a finger, clamped his own mouth over the journalist's, and blew hard. He hadn't a clue what this might achieve, but he'd seen a chap do it to someone half drowned in a film.

It was probably just luck, but it worked straight away. Josh was just bending to try a second blow when the journalist gargled and coughed up some horrible slime. *Glad my mouth wasn't there*, he thought. 'Hello,' he said aloud. 'Can you hear me?'

Palgrave opened his eyes. 'Yes, I can. Something hit me—was it *you*?'

'No, it was *that*.' Josh nodded towards the branch. 'Listen, can you get up, 'cause we'll both freeze to death if you don't.'

The journalist smiled crookedly. 'Sounds like a poor choice to me, son. Here goes.' He lifted his head, winced, and sat up.

Josh was hugely relieved. He'd had visions of running to the phone box by the bus shelter to dial 999. *Can* you call 999 without money? He didn't know, and anyway it didn't matter now. Palgrave was up on his feet, looking dazed.

'Where d'you want to *be*?' asked Josh. 'Only I've got to get home, my mum'll be having kittens.'

The man nodded. 'The pub . . . you

know . . . the whatsitsname?'

'Fox and Grapes?'

'That's it. I think I can manage, if you want to cut along.'

'No, no.' Josh shook his head. 'It's the same direction, I might as well see you on your way, but let's go.'

The wind was fiercer now. It roared in the elms, and drove snow like shrapnel into their faces as they battled up Shadows Lane. Conversation was near impossible, but a bruised journalist with a headache is still a journalist.

'The shopkeeper,' he yelled. 'Where was he trying to get to with those supplies?'

Josh was tired, but not *that* tired. He shrugged. 'Search me. One of his customers, I expect.'

'I thought everybody knew everybody else in a village.'

'No. There's loads of people I don't know in Coney Cley.'

'So what were *you* doing in Shadows Lane on a filthy night like this, son?'

'Saving your life, Mr Palgrave.'

'Yes, you certainly did that, and

don't think I'm not grateful because I am, but . . .'

'Why were *you* down there, Mr Palgrave?'

'I was doing my job, son—looking for a story.'

'There's no story down Shadows Lane, Mr Palgrave—just shadows. This is where I turn off.' They'd reached the top of Glebe Lane. 'Can you manage from here?'

The journalist nodded. 'Yes.' He looked at Josh. 'I'm glad we met this evening, son: if we hadn't, they'd have found me there tomorrow morning, dead.'

Josh nodded. 'Will you do one thing for me, Mr Palgrave?'

'Of course.'

'When you write the story of tonight, don't put me in it. My name, I mean: I'm not supposed to be here.'

Palgrave smiled. 'That's a promise, though *I* think you deserve a medal.' He grinned. 'Now wouldn't *that* make a story? G'night, Josh.'

'G'night, Mr Palgrave.'

FIFTY

NO PRESSURE

The branch that had felled Palgrave
had driven the box of rations into the
snow, so Josh hadn't seen it. What with
rescuing the journalist, and getting
back indoors without his mother
knowing he'd been out, he'd had little
time to think. It wasn't till he was
telling his sister the story in her room
and Jinty said, 'So old Manders
delivered the stuff and got home
before you arrived on the scene?' that
he realized this was probably not what
had happened.

He looked at her. 'He *can't* have, can
he, Sis? That drift's massive: Mr
Palgrave didn't get through, and
neither did I. And we weren't carrying
a box. Manders must've turned back.'

'Which means,' said Jinty, 'that
Boney didn't get his stuff.'

She was right. Saul Manders had
been back at the shop by twenty to five,

deeply worried. He talked the matter over with his wife. They agreed that it was unrealistic to hope for a rapid thaw tomorrow, and that Paul Bluet must have used up most of last week's meagre rations by now. 'He's nothing but skin and bone,' fretted Mrs Manders. 'His body's got no reserve of fat. Something's got to be done *now* or he'll just fade away.'

Saul Manders picked up the phone and called PC Lassiter. 'Norbert, it's Saul. Shadows Lane's completely blocked. I've tried, and I can't deliver Bluet's provisions. We're afraid he won't last long without them. Also, there's a nosy stranger about.'

'So, no pressure then,' chuckled the policeman. 'Look, Saul—obviously I can't come up with anything this minute. I'll phone the vicar, ask him to meet us this evening. Doctor Cruikshank too, if he can. Would you be free to come?'

'Of course.'

*   *   *

The meeting began at half-past seven, at the vicarage. Present were Mr and Mrs Manders, PC Lassiter, Dr Cruikshank and the vicar. These five were the only people in Coney Cley who knew the secret of Cornflower Cottage, apart from the six children. The vicar had a radical suggestion.

'We've kept Mr Bluet's secret splendidly,' he said. 'The village knows nothing about its shy guest in Shadows Lane, but I think the time has come to tell the villagers about him.'

'No.' The doctor shook his head. 'Paul Bluet's reason is very fragile. His eventual recovery may well depend on his being able to maintain the isolation he came here to find.'

The vicar nodded. 'I appreciate that, Doctor, but there'll be no eventual recovery if the poor fellow starves to death in the next few days.'

'That much is obvious,' said Doctor Cruikshank, 'but I fail to see how telling the villagers is going to solve the problem of getting food to him. I'd have thought a snowplough was what was needed, or even an air-drop.'

'You're absolutely right, of course,' conceded the vicar. 'Snag is, it'll take days or even weeks to get the use of a plough *or* a plane.' He smiled. 'What I have in mind is a great number of people with shovels.'

Mrs Manders looked at him. 'You mean, the *villagers*?'

The vicar nodded. 'Certainly, why not? It could happen tomorrow, but the people would have to know what they're digging *for*. If the meeting agrees, I'll make an announcement from the pulpit at morning service.'

The meeting agreed.

FIFTY-ONE

TEETH ON THE PILLOW

Sunday morning. Paul Bluet cracked open the front door and checked the step. There was no box. He'd sat up till ten last night, waiting for Manders, and it was ridiculous to think the grocer might have come and gone while he slept.

153

He knew he had *slept*, because of the dream. It was a dream in which he wakes to find all his teeth on the pillow. It wasn't the first time he'd had this dream. Starvation loosens the teeth: he'd started losing them in Kapowice, and more had dropped out here. He'd less than half a set now. He thought it didn't bother him much, but it must, deep down, to make him keep having the dream.

What bothered him this morning was not a shortage of teeth, but of something to get them into. He was keeping more of his food down lately, and last week's box was now empty except for two small potatoes and a piece of bread. It was still snowing, and there was no way of knowing when, if ever, more supplies might reach him. He had half a packet of tea, but when he tried to fill his kettle at the kitchen sink, he found that the pump was frozen. Neither gas nor electricity had ever been connected to the cottage. Bluet lit an oil lamp and stood it near the pump, in the hope that this might thaw it out. To get a cup of tea in the meantime, he'd have to collect a kettleful of snow to

154

melt on the stove.

It's all my own fault, *he told himself.* I ought to have moved as soon as the first snow fell. The Fox and Grapes. Manders suggested it. I'd have been no trouble to anybody there. As it is, he's having to trek through drifts and blizzards every Saturday to keep me fed, and those who know I'm here are burdened with my secret. How do I know Manders isn't lying out there somewhere, frozen to death because of me?

He stood at the open door for a while, swaddled in a blanket. The rhododendrons sagged under deep mantles of snow. Elsewhere the garden was an unbroken expanse of white, overlaid with a crust of glinting frost. Nothing moved except the drifting cloud of his breath. There was no sound.

Beautiful, *he thought.* No wire, no towers, no dogs. *He sighed and went in to boil a potato, the ghost of a smile hovering over his lips.*

FIFTY-TWO

A DIFFERENT SORT OF SERVICE

Not every villager went to St Hilda's on a Sunday morning, or at any other time. The Methodists had their own chapel, the nearest Catholic church was at Stowmarket, and there were some in Coney Cley who preferred to celebrate the Sabbath with a nice long lie-in.

It wasn't a bad congregation, though, considering conditions underfoot. Reverend Pike smiled down on it from the pulpit, rubbing his hands together to generate warmth.

'I intend to keep this morning's service brief,' he announced. 'One hymn, one prayer and no sermon.'

A rumble of surprise and curiosity rose to the vaulted ceiling. 'Surely to God they've not gone and put sermons on the ration?' asked a wit, none too quietly. There were chuckles, even though this was church.

The vicar pretended not to hear. 'There's a different *sort* of service to be rendered in Coney Cley today,' he continued. 'An urgent service, and one that will entail very hard work on behalf of a villager in distress. I feel sure that when you know of this villager, and learn the cause and nature of his distress, you will flock to join me at this service, bearing shovels in your hands and love in your hearts.'

Mrs Lassiter leaned towards Mrs Manders and whispered, 'Isn't he *wonderful*?'

Reverend Pike told the story of Paul Bluet, keeping it brief. Within ten minutes his listeners were streaming up the aisle, shaking his hand in the porch before stumping off to fetch something to dig with, and to rouse neighbours to do the same.

In the snow-clogged churchyard, Ken Roe intercepted an American serviceman he'd spotted among the worshippers. Nobody heard what passed between them, but there was arm-waving and head-shaking, culminating in an abrupt parting which didn't look all that friendly. None of Ken's classmates were there to witness this, and if they had they'd have thought it was just the swot, rubbing someone up the wrong way as usual.

FIFTY-THREE

EVER SUCH A QUEER STORY

Somebody knocked on the door as the Lintons were clearing away after a late breakfast. Jill opened it to find Mrs Lewis on the step with a shovel. She smiled. 'Come to clear our path, Bessie?'

Mrs Lewis shook her head. 'I've come straight from church,' she said. 'The vicar told us ever such a queer story, you'll never guess.'

Jill shook her head. 'Too cold to stand guessing, Bessie: come in and tell us.'

Josh pulled out a chair for their neighbour while Jinty made a fresh pot of tea. Their mother joined their guest at the table. 'Now, Bessie!' She smiled. 'What's this queer story of the vicar's?'

'It's about that old cottage at the bottom of Shadows Lane,' said Bessie.

Jinty nearly dropped the teapot. Josh looked startled, then blurted, 'Someone's living there.'

Mrs Lewis looked at him. 'How did you know—has someone been here before me?' His mother was looking at him too.

Josh shook his head. 'Nobody's been, Mrs Lewis. Me and Jinty've known for ages, but we promised not to tell. He's shy, you see, old Bo— Mr Bluet, I mean. Doesn't like people.' He frowned. 'Why's the vicar *telling* everyone?'

Mrs Lewis pulled a face. 'He's marooned, your Mr Bluet. Snowed in. They can't get food to him. Or coal, or anything. Vicar says he'll starve if we don't dig him out.'

'Dig him *out*?' gasped Jinty. 'Clear Shadows *Lane*, you mean? Surely that's impossible?'

Their neighbour shrugged. 'If it's impossible, the poor man's doomed,' she said flatly. 'I shouldn't be here drinking tea, I should be with Reverend Pike and the others.' She drained her cup and stood up. 'Will you join us? We're supposed to bring as many diggers as we can.'

Jill Linton looked dazed. 'My head's still in a whirl, Bessie. Can't believe my children knew about this and kept it to themselves.' She nodded. 'I'll come, though, of course I will.'

'We *all* will,' cried Jinty. 'Me and Josh've been *waiting* to make it up to Boney, and now's our chance.'

Josh looked at his sister. 'We've only got one shovel,' he said.

FIFTY-FOUR

IT'S OFF TO WORK WE GO

Reverend Pike's second service was better attended than his first. By eleven o'clock, the mouth of Shadows Lane looked like a gold rush. Shovels shushed and flew as a line of villagers dug their way into it, swivelling at the waist like miners to throw clots of snow behind them. This was pounced on at once by a squad of Coney Cley's strongest men, who piled it into wheelbarrows and tipped it onto the verges either side. The vicar smiled as he toiled, because his work-force included Methodists, Catholics and lots of people who weren't normally up yet, and they were all singing.

'Onward, Christian so-oldiers
Marching as to war . . .'

When Jinty and Josh arrived, Victor and the other wolves were there already. Wielding borrowed shovels, they formed a pack of five to help load barrows, and to start a rival song.

'Hi ho, hi ho,
It's off to work we go . . .'

Ever so slowly, the front line crept forward. Every now and then, PC Norbert Lassiter consulted his pocket-watch. He was worried. Winter days are short. In less than four hours it would be dark, and Shadows Lane had no lamps. It might be possible to continue, but progress was bound to slow as the the light faded and diggers grew tired.

The doctor glanced at him. 'What are our chances, Norbert?' He was breathing hard.

'Of reaching the cottage today?' The policeman pulled a face. 'Less than fifty-fifty I'd say, if we don't work on after dark.'

Cruikshank shook his head. 'People'll be done in by then, rations they're having to live on.'

Lassiter nodded. 'What about Bluet—think he can hang on if we don't break through till sometime tomorrow?'

The doctor sighed. 'Difficult to say. He survived worse in that camp, of course, but it weakened him terribly. And we don't know what food he's got, or how much coal, if any. We can only slog on and hope.'

At three o'clock the light started to fade. The line thinned as, one by one, diggers dropped out, exhausted. They'd got less than halfway. The singing stopped, and it began to snow.

FIFTY-FIVE

MIGHTY MACHINE

'. . . *with a shovel and a pick and a walking stick,*
Hi ho, hi-ho-hi-ho-hi—'

'That's *it*,' groaned Victor, straightening up. 'I'm all in.'

'Me too.' Donnie stuck his shovel in a snow heap and left it there so he could rub his back.

'Time is it?' panted Josh, leaning on his implement.

'Twenty past three,' grunted a barrowman. 'You kids quitting?'

Jinty nodded. ''Fraid so, mister. We're done for, and we wouldn't reach the cottage now, anyway.'

'No.' The man shook his head. 'We've done our best: you can't dig day and night on two ounces of bacon a week.'

'What about *Boney*, though?' protested Peter.

The barrowman frowned. '*Who?*'

'I mean, Mr Bluet. He's like a skeleton, he could be dead by tomorrow morning.'

'I know, lad, but like I said, we've done our best. Look.' He pointed. 'Everyone's stopping, even the— *Listen*—what's that?'

They listened. 'It's an engine,' murmured Victor. 'Reminds me of—'

'The *snowplough*!' cried Josh. 'The American one.' He punched the air. 'The *Yanks* are coming!'

They were. One Yank, anyway: the man who'd opened the Stowmarket Road a lifetime ago. As he rode his mighty machine down Shadows Lane, the exhausted diggers cheered and whooped, and when a file of DPs came trotting behind, they passed grinning under an arch of shovels lifted in their honour.

The wolves hugged one another, jumping up and down. 'How did they *know?*' cried Jinty, when they calmed down a bit.

'Dunno.' Victor frowned. 'Radar?'

'Radar nothing,' said a familiar voice. 'They knew 'cause *I* told 'em.'

'*You?*' Victor glowered at the swot. 'How could *you* have told them, twerp? You've been *here* all day.'

Ken shook his head. 'Not *all* day. I was in church, and so was an American officer. The vicar told everybody about Boney, and I collared the officer outside and asked him to send the plough.' He grinned. 'Never thought he *would*, though—told me to shove off.'

Victor nodded. 'He'd got taste, then. Anyway'—he punched the swot's arm—'you did all right for a sheep. Come *on.*'

The plough had moved further than the villagers had all day. From where the wolves stood, its outline was already hazy beyond a curtain of falling snow. Tiredness forgotten, they pelted after it, practising their howl.

FIFTY-SIX

WHAT ARE YOU, *CRAZY?*

'I say, can you . . . *hello*, can you stop here, please?' The vicar, above his knees in snow, stood right in front of the plough, waving.

'What the *heck* . . .?' The driver pulled up and stuck his head out. 'What are you, crazy? I could've driven right over you in the dark, you stupid son of a—' He noticed the dog collar and blushed. 'Gee, I'm sorry, Reverend, I didn't . . .'

Reverend Pike smiled. 'That's all right, soldier. I don't think we should take the plough too close to the cottage, though, because of the noise. Mr Bluet suffers from a nervous condition. One or two of us will proceed on foot the rest of the way, with his supplies.'

The American shrugged. 'Sure, if that's what you want.' He nodded towards the DPs, who'd stopped

166

shovelling to see what was happening. 'Take a coupla these characters along—they can clear the way and carry your stuff.'

'Thank you.' Pike went off to find Saul Manders, who'd brought a box of supplies when they'd expected to reach the cottage themselves. The soldier separated a pair of DPs from the squad and gave them instructions, using a mixture of bawled English and mime. One of the pair was Myron Pienkowski. When Pike returned with Manders, Pienkowski took the box, while his companion began digging a narrow pathway towards Cornflower Cottage, just visible through whirling flakes.

The wolves stood in a knot nearby, observing. Josh called out to the vicar. 'Can one of *us* come, sir? There's something we want to say to Mr Bluet.'

Reverend Pike shook his head. 'Not just now, laddie.' He smiled. 'Four strangers will be more than enough company for our unhappy guest, I fancy.' He turned towards those villagers who had not yet straggled off home. 'Bless you all,' he said. 'Today's was a fine and a selfless deed, demonstrating that there are more Good Samaritans in Coney Cley than Priests and Levites.'

He turned and set off along the narrow path, with Myron Pienkowski at his heels. Saul Manders brought up the rear, or would have if the four wolves, Ken and Jinty hadn't started after him, hoping he wouldn't glance back.

FIFTY-SEVEN

TOVARICH

Sound travels at night in a quiet place. Paul Bluet had heard the snowplough. It was a Russian tank, come at last to burst open the gates of Kapowice. The day he'd clung to life for was here.

When the knock came, he stumbled sobbing along the passageway and flung open the door. *'Tovarich!'* he choked, falling into the arms of the man standing there. *'Comrade.'*

The vicar embraced the trembling

sack of bones. 'It's all right, Paul,' he soothed. 'The war's over, you're in your grandfather's cottage, we've brought supplies.'

'Uh?' Bluet let go and stepped back, shaking his head. 'I . . . sorry, I get flashbacks, I heard a tank, thought it was the Red Army.' He wiped his eyes with the sleeve of the jacket he wore. 'We waited so long for the Red Army, most of us died.'

'I know,' said Reverend Pike softly. 'Or rather, I *don't* know: I've only seen pictures. It must have been dreadful beyond belief.' He nodded towards Manders, who was shining a torch on the step. 'You've seen Saul Manders before, haven't you? He's been fetching your box on Saturdays.' The grocer moved the beam to illuminate his own face.

Bluet peered and nodded. 'Yes,' he croaked. 'Thank you.'

'And the gentlemen behind him are displaced persons, working at the American base. This one kindly dug a path for us, and that one carried the box.'

As the torchlight swung to the surly DP, Bluet uttered a ghastly moan and crumpled. Before the vicar could catch him he fell to the floor, striking his head with a sound like an apple splitting.

Reverend Pike knelt and lifted the bleeding head, cradling it in his lap. 'Saul,' he rapped, 'go and see if the doctor's still here.' The grocer turned and he called after him, 'If not, send a boy to fetch him.'

The wolves, lurking under the rhododendrons, ducked back as Manders hurried by. 'What's happening?' hissed Peter. 'Is something wrong with Boney?'

Victor shook his head. 'Not sure. The vicar was talking to him, then he vanished and so did the vicar. Look out!'

One of the DPs was coming. The youngsters hid as the man scurried past, looking shaken. When he'd gone, Josh said, 'Manders knows what's going on, let's go ask him.'

The DP was now pushing through the hedge. He looked nervous, even from behind. They hung back till he was through, and were about to follow when Dr Cruikshank appeared. They crouched under snow-laden branches, holding their breath as doctor and grocer passed, heading for the cottage.

'Boney must be taken ill,' whispered Jinty. 'We better scarper before it gets any busier.'

Her brother nodded. 'Yeah you're right, Sis. Don't suppose we can do anything anyway. Come on.'

As the six emerged on Shadows Lane, the driver hailed them from his cab. 'Hey, kids—d'you know what's *happening* in there?'

Victor shrugged. 'We think Mr Bluet's been taken ill.'

The soldier nodded. 'I know *that* much—I heard the store clerk tell the doctor. What I want to know is, do they need me to wait with the truck, or can I get these guys the hell back to base?' He jerked his head towards the DPs, who were smoking and talking among themselves.

Pienkowski stood apart, gazing towards the cottage and fidgeting, as well he might. Pienkowski wasn't his real name, nor had he been a forced labourer for the Nazis. That name and occupation appeared on the forged papers he'd presented to the Americans. Those papers had cost Myron a great deal—and they were all that stood between him and the gallows.

'We don't know, sir,' said Jinty. 'We weren't supposed to be there.' She frowned. 'I suppose if Mr Bluet needed to go to hospital . . .'

'OK, OK.' The American nodded. 'I'll give it a few more minutes.' He smiled ruefully. 'It's all right for you guys, you're going home now. Me, I'm parbly gonna plough runways all night, and my home's three and a half thousand miles that way.' He jabbed a finger towards the west. 'G'night, kids.'

'Goodnight, sir.' Jinty smiled. 'Oh— and thanks for coming.'

FIFTY-EIGHT

YOU COULD WRITE A BOOK

Cruikshank and Manders carried the half-conscious Bluet to his bed in a corner of the kitchen, while the remaining DP stoked up the stove. The grocer wetted a cloth at the sink, and the doctor used it to dab away blood from the patient's scalp.

'Shine your torch just here,' he told Manders, 'and hold it steady.'

He examined the wound. 'It looks worse than it is,' he murmured, 'which is often the way with scalp wounds. Still, I'd like to have him in hospital under observation, at least till tomorrow.'

'No.' Bluet rolled his head from side to side on the blood-stained pillow. 'No hospital.'

'You banged your head on a stone floor,' protested Cruikshank. 'You may be concussed.'

Bluet smiled, the smile of a skull. 'It

was banged more than once at Kapowice, Doctor. Sometimes it was banged for me by others, but I was never under observation, except from the guard-towers. And I'm making sense, aren't I: not rambling or anything?'

The doctor shook his head. 'Not now, but you were a few minutes ago. What was it—something about a butcher?'

'Ah.' Bluet seemed to recall something. 'That's right, I thought I saw . . .' He shook his head. 'Doesn't matter, it was a flashback, like the tank and the Russian soldier.' He smiled faintly. 'You'd be amazed what I see, Doctor: people dead in Poland, who come to watch me eat. You could write a book.'

Cruikshank smiled. 'Perhaps I will someday, but in the meantime, if you definitely won't go into hospital, I propose to stay here overnight to keep my eye on you.' He glanced up at Manders. 'You get off, Saul—you and our friend here.' He indicated the DP. 'The Yank'll probably drop you off.'

'But what if your patient deteriorates in the night? There's no telephone here: the closest is the kiosk on the Green.'

The doctor smiled. 'Let's cross that bridge when we come to it, shall we? Goodnight, Saul.'

'Well—if you're sure . . . goodnight, Ewan, goodnight, Paul.'

FIFTY-NINE

LIKE A SORT OF BADGE

When the six kids reached the top of Shadows Lane, PC Lassiter was there, talking to Brian Palgrave. 'That's him,' said the reporter, nodding towards Josh. 'The chap who saved my life.'

Lassiter nodded. 'I know young Joshua, he's a good lad.' He looked at the youngsters. 'Can you kids hang on a minute? I know you've had a hard day, but I'd like a quick word.' He turned back to Palgrave, dropping his voice so the children wouldn't hear. 'As I was saying, the police can make a man's life difficult in all sorts of ways if they choose to, and they're not overly fond of reporters at the best of times. So all in all, it might be best if you steer clear of Coney Cley for a month or two. Nothing's happening here that your readers need to know about anyway. Do you receive my meaning?'

Palgrave snorted. 'Obviously, but where does that leave the freedom of the press?'

'It leaves it where the press leaves people's right to privacy, sir.'

The reporter spun on his heel and strode away, seemingly furious. The policeman watched him go, then turned to the wolves. 'Now then, kids, I've a nice little job for you if you're willing to take it on.'

They looked at him. 'What sort of job?' asked Victor.

'Not one you'd need the School Certificate for. See the path you've cleared today, right down to Cornflower Cottage?'

'Yes, we've just walked up it.'

'Well, how d'you feel about walking

up it every afternoon, straight from school?'

'What *for*?'

'To keep it open. Just a narrow path, so Mr Manders and the doctor can get down and back on foot.'

They looked at one another, then at PC Lassiter. 'All right, we'll do it,' agreed Jinty. 'Should be fun. Do we tell our mums you asked us to?'

'Certainly.' He looked serious. 'There are a few rules, though.'

'What rules?'

'Rule one, no going into Mr Bluet's garden. Rule two, no prehistoric noises. Rule three, you must trample the snow well down each time, not just leave footprints. And rule four, it's to be just the six of you, not every kid in the blessed school: this isn't a game. Agreed?'

They all nodded.

'Good. Start tomorrow. And let me know *straightaway* if ever you can't get through, so we can think of something else. All right?'

'All right.'

'*I* know,' chirped Donnie, when

they'd left the policeman behind. 'We can wear our wolf masks, like a sort of badge. You know—*wolves only.*'

'I haven't *got* a mask,' grumbled Jinty. 'Nor has Ken.'

'Yes, you *have*,' laughed her brother. 'Difference is, yours don't come off.'

SIXTY

MR PIERREPOINT'S TRAP DOOR

The man known as Myron Pienkowski was afraid. He'd been afraid three years ago, hiding in the Polish forest, wearing clothes he'd stripped from a corpse. He'd fled the camp at Kapowice as the Russian army drew near, leaving his SS guard's uniform in some bushes. He'd been Stepan Bilciuk back then—Butcher Bilciuk to the wretched prisoners he'd terrorized for two and a half years—and if the Reds had caught him he'd have been tried at Kharkov and hanged as a murderer.

He'd slipped away, given himself a

new name and joined the thousands of refugees on Poland's dusty roads. After weeks of tramping, he'd been admitted to a displaced persons' camp under his false name, and when the war ended he'd been recruited by the US military as a labourer. Shipped to England he'd believed himself safe, his brutal past buried for ever.

No longer. He sat with his fellow DPs in the bed of the bouncing truck, replaying in his mind the scene that had brought back his fear. The cottage door opening. The emaciated figure throwing itself at the priest, croaking 'Tovarich'. Bilciuk spoke no English, but he knew the Russian for 'comrade'. The light from the doorway was feeble and he was standing well back. It might have been all right if the stupid priest hadn't made the shopkeeper shine his torch on him. Bluet's instantaneous, terrified reaction made it obvious to Bilciuk that the man had recognized him, and although Bilciuk did not recognize Bluet, he knew by the man's condition that he could only be a camp survivor.

Damn and blast, said Bilciuk to himself. *What were the odds against my finding a Kapowice survivor in England, of all places? And out of all the DPs at Coney Cley Base, why did they pick me for this snow-clearing detail? It's a million to one chance, and it's left me standing right on Mr Pierrepoint's trap door with a rope round my neck.* He gripped the edge of the tin seat with both hands and shook his head. *I won't hang, not after all I've been through. Only Bluet can identify me, and I won't stand by and let him do it.*

He smiled tightly in the dim truck. *I missed the chance to eliminate him in Kapowice: this time there'll be no mistake.*

SIXTY-ONE

A SHEET OF WHITE VELVET

It had frozen hard on Sunday night and snowed most of Monday, so that when the wolves gathered at the top of

Shadows Lane after school, there were three inches of fresh snow to be trampled. Ken wasn't there—he'd had to stay home and help his mum.

The four boys donned the masks they'd kept hidden all day in their satchels. Jinty looked at them and grinned. 'They're really good, you know. Miss Bowman's a genius. Wonder where she got the stuff?'

'She told my mum it was an old coat,' said Peter. 'Fake fur, looks real.'

Jinty nodded. 'It certainly does. You look more like wolves than wolves.'

'You're jealous,' accused her brother.

'Yes I am, but never mind. I can trample snow, which is what we're here for. Come on.'

The boys loped in pairs for a wider track. Jinty followed, stamping down bits they missed. It was dark, but the snow had stopped and there were stars. The evidence of yesterday's work lay muffled, as if somebody had thrown a sheet of white velvet over it.

With the great drift gone, it took only a few minutes to reach the gateway of Cornflower Cottage. The five stood in a half-circle round it, their breath pluming about their heads. The snow here was undisturbed, it seemed nobody had passed in or out for some hours, and the cottage itself was almost invisible beyond rhododendrons like gigantic cauliflowers, bowed by their burdens of snow.

'We didn't howl,' complained Donnie.

'Well, you're not howling *here*,' Victor told him. 'Rule two, remember?'

'Yeah, so what *are* we doing?'

'We're not doing *anything*, dummy. Rule four, this isn't a game. We tramp back, go home, remember to howl tomorrow.'

'Well, I'm disappointed. I mean, here's us in these terrifying masks, and there's nobody to scare. It's a waste.'

Jinty shook her head. 'Don't talk tripe, Donnie. Mr Lassiter didn't recruit us to scare people, he recruited us to keep the track open. You didn't expect to meet people down here, surely?'

'Ssssh!' Victor pressed a finger to his

lips. 'I didn't, but here comes somebody anyway.'

SIXTY-TWO

DISTINCTLY GREEN

As the wolves listened to the approach of a person or persons unknown, Manders and Reverend Pike knocked on the door of the police house and were admitted.

'What's up?' asked Constable Lassiter, when the three of them had taken seats in the front room that doubled as a police station.

'Maybe nothing,' said the vicar. 'It's just . . . Saul and I are uneasy about something that happened yesterday at Cornflower Cottage.'

'Oh?' The policeman arched his brow. 'I hoped we'd sorted all that out. Doctor Cruikshank says Paul Bluet had a restful night and seems none the worse for his fainting fit. I've got some kids tramping Shadows Lane after school each day to keep a pathway open, and the inquisitive stranger'll be sent packing next time I see him.'

The vicar nodded. 'It's the fainting fit we're worried about, Norbert. Not so much the faint itself, as what brought it on.'

'What d'you think *did* cause it? Cruikshank says it was panic—the poor chap thought he was back in the camp.'

Manders shook his head. 'We think he saw somebody. Somebody he recognized. Somebody who frightened him so badly he passed out.'

Lassiter shrugged. '*Who*, though? There were the two of you and Cruikshank, nobody else.'

'The doctor wasn't there when Paul fainted,' said Manders, 'but two DPs were.'

'Ah,' said the policeman. 'Didn't know about those. Harmless though, surely? Pair of foreigners he can't ever have seen before.'

'That's just it,' said Pike. 'We're wondering if he *had* seen one of them before. At Kapowice, perhaps.'

'Another prisoner? Big coincidence,

but why should it make him faint?'

The vicar shook his head. 'Not another prisoner. A guard.'

Lassiter pulled a face. 'Can't see the Yanks employing a former concentration camp guard, can you?'

'They might not *know*. There are such things as forged papers, stolen identities.'

'Thing is,' put in Manders, 'one of those chaps looked distinctly green around the gills after Paul collapsed. Hurried off into the rhododendrons. I think he was terrified.'

'Of Paul Bluet?'

'Of being unmasked. There are a lot of former guards on the run, you know, including some of the most sadistic ones.'

'Hmmm.' The policeman thought about this. 'Tell you what I'll do,' he said. 'I'll phone the base commander, say we're suspicious of one of his DPs. You don't happen to know the chap's name, I suppose?'

Both men shook their heads. 'Say it was the one the driver sent to carry the box of groceries,' said Pike.

'Why don't we just ask Paul?' suggested Manders. 'I know he needs privacy and all that, but it can't be doing him much good if he knows one of his former guards is stationed down the road.'

Lassiter nodded. 'You're absolutely right, Saul. In fact, I think I'll pop down there now. I can check on the kids' work at the same time. Anybody want to come along?'

Both men did.

SIXTY-THREE

THE FORMER SUPERMAN

'P'raps it's the doctor?' suggested Peter. 'Come to check on Boney.'

'Or Constable Lassiter, come to check on *us*,' growled Donnie. They strained their eyes towards the soft beat of boots on snow. The newly risen moon slipped from behind a cloud, flooding the lane with cold light.

Jinty gasped. 'It looks like that DP—

you know, the one who looked scared when he passed us in the bushes.'

'What the heck's *he* doing here?' murmured Josh.

'Haven't a clue,' whispered Victor. 'He's so busy staring at the ground he hasn't spotted us. We could hide in the garden and see what he does.'

One by one they slipped through the gateway. Once through they turned sharp right, following the line of the hedge, crouching in its shadow. Nobody spoke, or even breathed. They could hear the man shuffling about, muttering to himself. After a few seconds he appeared in the gateway and stood, gazing towards the cottage. As the five watched, the DP opened his long coat and drew out a knife. Moonlight shone dully on its short blade. Transferring the weapon to his left hand, he advanced, disappearing into the rhododendrons.

The youngsters looked at one another. A bit of excitement's one thing. Spying at night in a lonely spot on a foreigner who's got a dagger is another.

Josh swallowed. Could he be a hero now, like his dad? He really, really wanted to. '*Now* what?' he croaked.

Victor cleared his throat. 'He's after Boney, isn't he? *Must* be. We need the police, but he'd have got him by the time—'

The dagger man must have reached the front door—they heard him knock.

'We could howl,' said Josh huskily, who really only wanted to run away.

The other boys lifted their hands to touch their masks. They'd forgotten they were wearing them. The man was knocking again, harder.

'Boney isn't answering,' murmured Jinty. 'P'raps the man'll give up, go away.'

Victor shook his head. 'No, he won't. He's come all this way, he'll get in somehow.' He looked at Josh. 'Good idea of yours, howling, only not here. Remember when we saw the statue?'

Josh nodded.

'We were dead scared, weren't we?'

They all nodded.

'Well—what if we howl near the statue, and this character comes to

188

investigate and sees the statue under the moon with a pack of wolves around it?'

Peter pulled a face nobody could see. 'He's an adult with a knife, chum. He's been in a war, seen stuff. He's not going to be scared off by a bunch of kids in masks.'

There came a noise of glass breaking. 'Told you,' rapped Victor. 'He's going to climb through a window. It might not work, the statue idea, but it's all we've got. Come *on*.'

He led them under laden rhododendrons, up to the corner and along the side of the cottage. Sounds reached them: snarls and gasps, a tinkling. The man was plucking shards of glass from a window frame. Josh wondered what he could possibly want with Boney.

When the first thin howl rose on the frosty air, Stepan Bilciuk whirled, catching his palm on a fang of glass. *What the—?* He hunched forward, grimacing, his right hand clamped to the bleeding palm of his left. As the first howl shivered away, another rose, then a third. Fragments of jumbled thoughts seethed inside his head. *No wolves, this is England. What, then? Dogs. Must be dogs. Of course, dogs, but where? Are there men . . . men with these dogs?* Working at the window, he'd stuck the knife down his belt. Now he drew it with his sticky right hand, pointed it towards the cacophony which seemed to come from behind the cottage. Blood was dripping from his gashed palm, sprinkling the snow. He moved along the side of the house, cursing, holding the knife out in front of him, till he came in sight of the lawn. The sight that met his eyes there made him moan with fear.

He'd been a soldier of the dreaded SS: a strutting superman with the power of life and death over thousands of lesser men, but all the time, underneath the swagger and the uniform had lurked the real Stepan Bilciuk: a deeply ignorant country bumpkin, his sluggish mind inhabited by a phantasmagoria of horrifying ghosts which had haunted his ancestors for centuries.

Now he saw, in the middle of the moonwashed lawn, a female spirit. Around her, gazing balefully straight at him, stood a half-circle of creatures he recognized, but had never seen till now.

Werewolves.

The knife fell from Bilciuk's hand. As Jinty watched from behind the statue, the former superman turned with a shuddering groan and fled. And when he reached the top of Shadows Lane and saw the grocer, the vicar and the policeman, he threw himself, gibbering, into their arms.

SIXTY-FOUR

NOT SO BONEY

They say bad things always come in threes, but sometimes the opposite is true: one good thing'll happen, then another, and just when you think life can't possibly get any better, along comes a third.

It was like that in Coney Cley, a few days after the hangman sent Stepan Bilciuk to join his victims.

It was a Saturday in early April. The long, long winter had finally relaxed its grip, and the sun was busy zapping the last traces of snow along the lines of walls and hedge-bottoms. That was the first good thing.

With no more trampling to do, the four wolves gathered on the Green to sit in the bus shelter and watch the world go by. They didn't see it, because the world never came through Coney Cley. In fact, the world had never even *heard* of the place. A man came by, though: a thin man with scarecrow hair, who nodded at the boys and treated them to a toothless smile.

'He's not so boney these days,' said Victor, following the man with his eyes.

'No.' Josh shook his head. 'He'll run to fat if he's not careful.' The others laughed, and that was the second.

Jinty missed this, because she'd gone to call for her best friend, Sandra Tasker. As Paul Bluet passed from view, the two girls came tripping across

192

the grass, holding hands and grinning like lunatics.

'What's up with *you* two?' demanded Josh. 'You look as if you lost a ha'penny and found a fiver.'

'Better than that,' Jinty smiled. 'Janet's coming home.'

'Who the heck's *Janet*?' growled Peter.

'My sister,' said Sandra. 'You know: she married a Yank.'

'And is the Yank coming too?' asked Donnie, who liked Yanks because of the Zippos and gum and other fancy stuff they were apt to spread around.

Sandra shook her head. 'No, she left him. They didn't get on, and anyway she was missing Mum and me.' She grinned broadly. 'Week on Wednesday, we're off to Southampton to meet her ship.'

And that was the third.

When the two girls had moved on, the wolves crossed the road and turned right into Glebe Lane. The school gates stood open, and a lorry was parked at the kerb.

'What's going on over there?' asked

Josh.

They were about to cross and investigate when Ken Roe came out of the churchyard.

Victor groaned and called out, 'What you been doing, Swot—choosing your grave?'

'No, yours. Have you seen what they're doing in the schoolyard?'

'Who?'

'Council. Go look.'

'We were about to. See you Monday then, eh?' Victor didn't want Ken tagging along.

The Swot shook his head. 'No, you won't, we're moving.'

They looked at him. *'Moving?'* asked Donnie. *'Where?'*

'Stowmarket. My mum's not risking another winter stuck here. Stowmarket's civilized, she says.'

'Yeah, so why spoil it by taking *you* there?' joked Victor.

Ken ignored him. 'Cheerio, bumpkins,' he said. 'Enjoy your new shelter.' And he walked away, whistling.

Four men in overalls were working

on the former air-raid shelter. There were three ragged holes in its front wall where they'd knocked bricks out.

'Bit rough, isn't it?' said Victor. 'Are you *leaving* it like that?'

'Shove off, you cheeky young blighter,' snarled one of the men. 'It's none of your business.'

'It *is*, actually,' contradicted Victor. 'I'm the design consultant on this job.'

'Oh aye, and I'm the Archduke of Abyssinia.' The workman turned his back on the boys, who strolled along to inspect the rest of the structure.

On the side was another hole, beautifully squared off with wet cement. Victor wrote in it with a finger while the others kept a lookout. Nobody noticed the inscription for days, and by then the cement was rock-hard. It read:

THE HAMMOND SHELTER OPENED APRIL 1947 BY MR VICTOR HAMMOND, DESIGN CONSULTANT

Spring came, as it always does. The

wolfpack disbanded itself. The baby clinics continued, and the whist-drives. Queen Anne's lace bloomed cream along the roadsides, to be replaced in August by fireweed.

Nothing ever happens in Coney Cley.

GLOSSARY

Beano, p. 56
Weekly comic paper, still published.

Becher's Brook, p. 53
One of the most difficult jumps in the annual Grand National horse race

Bull's-eye, p. 11
Large round boiled sweet: gob-stopper.

Coupon, p. 9
Dated stamp in ration book, to be surrendered in exchange for weekly ration of fats, meat, sugar etc.

Captain Oates, p. 144
Intrepid Anatarctic explorer, who died in 1912 on the Scott expedition.

DPs
Displaced Persons.

Final Solution, p. 105
Nazi project to exterminate all Jews, gipsies and other 'undesirable' peoples in Europe.

Gurn or Girn, p. 45
To pull an ugly face.

Hotspur, p. 102
Weekly comic for boys.

Larry Olivier, p. 94
Sir Laurence Olivier, famous actor.

Liquorice root, p. 5
Dried root of liquorice plant, sold to children when sweets were rationed. Chewed, it yielded a sweetish juice. Horrible.

M. R. James, p. 43
Renowned writer of horror stories.

Mairzy Doats, p. 49
Novelty song of the late forties.

Mr Pierrepoint, p. 178
Public hangman 1930s–60s

Rats of Hamelin, p. 56
Featured in a poem by Robert Browning—'The Pied Piper of Hamelyn'.

SS, p. 178
Schutz Staffel—Hitler's feared army of black-uniformed troops. Some committed grisly atrocities or staffed concentration camps.

Sunny Stories, p. 2
Weekly paper of stories by Enid Blyton.

Vera Lynn, p. 94
Favourite singer of the War years.

Whist-drive, p. 9
A social activity with card-playing for small prizes.